Intr

John Costin in ~~your~~ ...
creative, mission-focuseu

John has a rare gift of understanding people of different nationalities and cultures and finding common ground. His disarmingly-gentle demeanor, charm and quick smile (which hide an underlying toughness) eliminate any risk of being viewed as dominant or threatening. People instinctively like and trust him.

They are among his most positive attributes. They brought him success in a corporation where fighting the bureaucracy was often like walking in solidifying concrete. He never gives up. It helped him conquer his serious illness. Years from now, when his time is finally up, he'll negotiate a better position for himself in Heaven...and St. Peter will sign.

Bob Lutz
Former Vice Chairman
General Motors

To my best friend
Steve one of the
very best people
in the world
I love you

John

October 23 2018

Praise for John Costin and
Unleash Your Potential

"Management by Encouragement is by far the most effective management style I experienced during more than 25 years of experience in the Automotive Industry. Most managers intuitively believe that criticizing their team members and working on their weaknesses generates results. However, encouraging people to take risks and make mistakes turned out to be far more effective.

Management by encouragement means reinforcing people's strengths and encouraging them to do the unexpected. I experienced myself with John Costin as my leader that this leadership style was a true booster of self-esteem and positive thinking. It drove me to step outside of my comfort zone and to take far more risk with the most positive attitude...generating great results.

Encouragement means leadership trust and backing in case of trouble, both aspects are critical enablers especially for young talents to explore new grounds and to work outside of organizational hierarchies and boundaries. It also means charging young talents with tasks they initially believe they can never accomplish. Whenever they succeed...and they will do...their motivation goes through the roof."

- *Imelda Labbe, Head of Global Group, Aftersales, Volkswagen, Germany*

"While working in John's organization, I had the privilege of witnessing first hand an inclusive yet decisive leadership style. His approach was unfailingly even-tempered not only during routine meetings but also when engaged in arduous discussions. Invariably, John had a knack for keeping his teams on track not only to arrive at difficult decisions but also to yield results his contemporaries and all whom he managed sought to emulate."

- *Kim Kurtz-Seslar, Engineering Group Manager - Type Approval/Certification and Export Regulations, General Motors, USA*

"I have had the pleasure to work for and with John. He is an astute businessman, able to handle complex structures and exceed expectations on targets and delivering high levels of profitability. He has a keen ability to rally teams together (including diverse multi-cultural groups), motivate them and obtain the best results. He has been a teacher, mentor and friend."

- *Robert C. Triulzi, Former General Director Aftermarket, Asia Pacific, Private Consultant and Global Automotive Executive, USA*

"Top executive with positive human approach!"

- *Armin Grond, Languages, Cultures CEO, Switzerland*

"John has something special that nobody has. He is so unique in his ways as he has an abundance of charisma and his approach in all things is refreshing and motivating. I have learned so much from John as he always leads by example. I have been fortunate enough to have worked with John since 2002. He is an engaging, enthusiastic born leader. A big problem is nothing when it comes to John. He has a style that is calming and reassuring as he always finds a solution to the problem. You can have many friends, but in this man, I have discovered a mentor, a leader, a business guru, and most importantly, a friend that I have learned to rely on and trust."

- *Paul Chedid, President, Paul Chedid Automotive Group, Paris, France*

ABOUT THE AUTHOR

John Costin has held numerous executive positions in the automotive industry internationally, throughout Europe and in the United States. He is the former Chairman and CEO of Delta Motor Group and credited with saving the Finish automotive company during the last global recession. He has held Executive positions in Opel Ag Germany, Vauxhall Motors UK, General Motors International and General Motors USA. Be it as a CEO, President or Executive Director, John's signature leadership style insures peak performance. He possesses unwavering leadership, international perspective and in-depth knowledge of every aspect of the automotive industry. John is currently President of HUMVEE EXPORT, LLC and President and owner of Around the World Business Consulting Services.

UNLEASH YOUR
POTENTIAL
A MANAGEMENT SERIES

JOHN COSTIN

UNLEASH YOUR POTENTIAL:
A MANAGEMENT SERIES
Fat Dog Books

Published by
Fat Dog Books
California, USA

Fat Dog Books
ISBN: 978-0-9991370-0-0

Business & Money/Management & Leadership
Printed in the United States of America

Visit our website at www.fatdogbooks.com

DEDICATION

I dedicate this book to Dr. Jenny Rise and a young man I eventually had the honor and pleasure of meeting - Constantin Braun.

Having been diagnosed with Acute Myeloid Leukemia (AML), I was recommended by Dr. Jenny Rise, a personal friend, to go for treatment at the Dana Farber hospital in Boston, Massachusetts, and it was there that I eventually received a stem cell transplant.

For months, I received treatment in preparation for the transplant of bone marrow stem cells from a twenty-three year old young man from Germany. It would be several years before I would be allowed to know the identity and location of my donor, as is the policy of the organization that found him - *Be the Match*. The important point is that his cells were a *perfect* match for me.

As I waited for the transplant, I wrote the outline of this book, from my hospital bed.

This unselfish young man gave me the cells that keep me alive today, and allow me to maintain a normal life. It was a very emotional day when we met for the very first time. Not many people come face-to-face with the person who saved their life.

I am eternally grateful to you Constantin.

ACKNOWLEDGEMENT

First and foremost, I would like to acknowledge my lovely wife, Marcella. I am blessed in so many ways but none more than having you by my side as my wife. Thank you for always being there every step of the way during my challenging times with your creativity, enthusiasm, perspective and love. You are the best.

James and Hannah, thank you for your support and for providing me with five wonderful grandchildren, Jemima, Erin, Connor, Molly and Megan.

Summer, my writing coach, I am grateful for your professionalism, grace and calm during the difficult time in my life. You made it all so much easier than it should have been.

Michael, my editor and publisher at Fat Dog Books, this wouldn't be possible without your belief in me.

CONTENTS

Book One

BARKERS ON MEETINGS

INTRODUCTION

My management career, at companies such as Vauxhall Motors UK, Opel Germany, Delta Motor Group Finland, General Motors Europe, General Motors International and General Motors USA, has led me to live and work in many different countries around the world. As a result, I've rubbed shoulders with people from six continents, encompassing a variety of cultures and workplace styles. Over time, I've gathered together a number of management tools that I've used and developed, which have worked for me in various countries and organizations. In a way, I have a management toolbox of my very own. When I move to a new assignment, if there is a need, I pull out a particular tool and introduce it to my new team, with mostly positive results.

Putting my toolbox concepts on paper, in a book, and sharing them with others, is an idea that came to me slowly and grew over the years. I recall sitting with good friends one winter, on high stools around a table in a warm and friendly pub, discussing what it's like doing business around the world. It was from this discussion, with people I respect and love, that the idea of a book was first hatched. I was explaining, in a humorous way, the different behaviors of people participating in meetings in various parts of the world. My intension was merely good conversation, but my companions, apparently, found deeper value in my words.

Several of my observations centered on the particularities of American meetings. I have to say that, while I truly appreciate the American way of doing business and the win-win attitude displayed in most meetings, there are times when it can be counterproductive. Americans seem to be encouraged, from an early age, to always participate in meetings and to make a contribution, even though they may not have read the necessary materials prior to the meeting. This conveys great enthusiasm, but often, in the end, it is not clear to everyone what has been agreed on among the chatter of contribution, or who is responsible for executing ideas that were discussed.

On the other hand, I explained to my friends, a meeting in Germany is entirely different. The participants will have read and researched the pre-meeting notes and arrived ready to argue the case based on the facts at hand. This compares with the more chess-like discussion in United Kingdom meetings where, even early on in the process, it is possible to detect personal positioning and strategy playing an important role in trying to guide participants in a certain direction without anyone clearly stating why.

A particularly interesting meeting style takes place in Japan. There, the layout of the room plays a very important role. The senior Japanese sit in a line facing the door, while the visitors sit on the other side, backs to the door, as the Japanese like to have first sight of any intruders. During meetings, Japanese businessmen tend to nod throughout. An inexperienced manager would believe that he or she was receiving positive signs of approval for the proposal being presented. Imagine the surprise when discovering, at the conclusion of the meeting, this is not the case. The nods were to illustrate an understanding of what was being said, not an approval.

During these discussions, my friends repeatedly pressed me to explain what I carried in my management toolbox to handle these differences. When I did, I was encouraged to put the concepts into a book, for others to learn from my experiences. Ultimately, I wrote the outline of this book, *Barkers on Meetings*, and it became the first in my three book *Unleash Your Potential* management series. It is written in a lighthearted way, although with a serious concept at its core. The book itself can be read in about an hour and gets at what is a major issue in small, medium and large companies in business today. *There are just too many meetings*, which often overlap and unnecessarily drain management's time. This book has a process to cure this bane of all management!

PART ONE: THE STORY

Deep in the heart of the Midwestern United States in St. Bernard, a city named after the famed explorer, Albert Saint Bernard, Bertie Boxer was preparing for his first day at his new job. He'd just arrived from Britain to be the new CEO of Barkers Incorporated, an international canine accessories company. Hired by the chairman of the board and unanimously endorsed at the last board meeting, Bertie had expectation heaped high on his shoulders.

Bertie was quite familiar with Barkers Inc. and had endeavored to become more so in preparation for his new job. Barkers was a grand old company, established over 100 years ago. It was headquartered in St. Bernard, but enjoyed a worldwide reputation. Unfortunately, like many companies, Barkers Inc. had fallen on hard times. This was due in part to the overall global economy, but also to a corporate culture that had grown stale, complacent, and stubbornly set in its ways. That culture, in fact, was what Bertie had been hired to change.

Bertie knew the best way to handle his new position was to establish his own opinions about the company and the personnel he would be leading. Looking in the mirror in his hotel room, he put aside all doubt and unwanted advice, and adjusted his favorite red tie. He withdrew a notepad and wrote himself a note, sticking it to the mirror. Nodding in satisfaction at the message, Bertie headed off to his first day at Barkers Inc.

There's something to hear in every dog's bark

All around St. Bernard, as Bertie was anticipating his day, various managers and staff of Barkers Inc. were also getting ready for work, each with their own ideas and hopes about what their new CEO from Britain would be like. One of these, Minnie Westie, the zealous K9 Resources Manager of Barkers, was particularly optimistic about the new CEO. Minnie, in fact, was optimistic about most things, a trait which served her well. She'd yet to meet a task that a little hard work and enthusiasm couldn't conquer, and she looked forward to the challenges a new boss would bring. Determined to impress and be noticed, Minnie put on her favorite bright bow and hurried off to work.

Minnie's longtime friend and coworker, Gary Golden, was much less confident he would like Boxer. Gary was normally an easygoing fellow, which was why he and Minnie got along well, but Gary was Head of Sales, and he feared he knew where the leash would be tightened in the struggling company. He bumbled around in his closet, worrying about his family, his big house, his prized bone collection and his comfortable job, while his wife got the little goldens ready for school.

Gary Golden had worked for Barkers for years. He started right out of college and he felt he'd earned the perks and stability he now enjoyed. A bit of a chow hound, Gary liked his lunches, his travel budget, his work dinners and his golf outings with clients. Gary didn't want a new boss. He didn't want anything to change. In his worry, he also didn't stop to consider that if nothing changed, soon no one would have a job at Barkers any longer.

A tail wag takes you further than a growl

In a nearby suburb of St. Bernard, Stella Scottie sat alongside her husband Stan while chomping on her breakfast. Stella, who was known for her bite as well as her bark, was Head of Manufacturing and Plant Operations at Barkers. Even more so than Gary Golden, Stella didn't like the idea of a new boss, especially one from Britain.

"What does a Boxer from Britain know about how to run one of the largest companies in the Midwest?" Stella snarled. "With my abilities to organize and coordinate everything at Barkers, I should have been made CEO. But no, I wasn't even a consideration."

Stan's tail quietly slid underneath him. He had heard this tirade before.

"I would have had the place making money in no time," Stella growled. "The first order of business would have been to reduce the tail count. Get rid of that useless Head of Sales, Gary Golden, for one. He eats more than he sells. And the next to go would be his useless, over-confident enabler, Minnie Westie."

Does every dog have only one day?

Stella Scottie continued her fit as she ate, expounding at length on all the mistakes she was sure the new CEO would make, until, by the time she left for work, she had developed an extensive list of reasons not to like him.

Not long after, when an enthusiastic Minnie, a fearful Gary and an obstinate Stella arrived at Barkers headquarters, they found that their new boss had arrived at work bright and early. In fact, Bertie Boxer had already sent out an email announcing a meeting for all the managers and supervisors of Barkers Inc.

Dear Managers and Supervisors at Barkers,

I would like you to join me in the main conference room today at 1:00 PM so I may introduce myself and have the opportunity to meet all of you. I ask that you free up your time to be with me the entire afternoon.

Directly following my introduction, I will be hosting a Meeting on Meetings. I am interested in how decisions are currently being made in this company. No preparations are necessary for this meeting. Please do not bring your computers, phones or papers to the conference room.

Sincerely,
Bertie Boxer
Chief Executive Officer
Barkers Inc.

Minnie Westie read the subject line, Meeting on Meetings, with her usual tail-wagging enthusiasm. She was sure this meeting would be the perfect opportunity for her to impress Bertie Boxer, and the rest of Barkers, with her business acumen and her can-do attitude. She formed a vision of how the meeting would go in her mind and of herself showing what an asset she was to Barkers.

Gary Golden hunkered down to read Boxer's email, his ears drooping. Gary knew that a new CEO meant changes. He was so worried about his perks, he didn't even think about what a meeting on meetings could accomplish, only about how much he would despise being forced to stand in front of the other managers and justify all his extra bones. Gary started to pace, certain that his worries were exactly what Bertie Boxer would make him do. Unlike Minnie, Gary was letting his fear shape his vision of the future.

> *Sometimes a steak is really a rubber chew toy*

Stella Scottie read Boxer's email with a sniff and a snarl, determined before she even opened it not to like it. She couldn't wait to get her paws on her phone, dialing up the other managers one by one to tell them what she thought of Bertie Boxer from Britain and his meeting on meetings.

"Why, even the subject is ridiculous," she snapped and snarled into the phone. "Doesn't he realize the deadlines we're all dealing with? We have enough meetings as it is. Holding a meeting about meetings is only a waste of every dog's time. If Barkers really wants to save money, they should ask me what to do. I definitely wouldn't start by having a meeting on meetings and getting every dog's fur up."

"And look at this," she barked. "We can't bring our laptops, phones or even papers. He means to give a long speech, I can tell already, and to make us sit through every word. What a waste of time. And it's obvious he plans on pitting us one against the other."

"Well, yes," said Lucia Lowchen, Head of Engineering, when Stella called her. "A meeting on meetings does sound silly. I couldn't agree more, Stella, such a waste of time. Still, can't stand up to the new boss, can we? If there's a meeting, we'll just have to go."

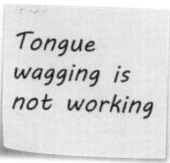

Tongue wagging is not working

Lucia hung up the phone, unconcerned. Out of all the managers, she knew she was best in show. She let the engineers on her team call the shots, keeping them happy while creating less work for herself. As engineers, they were all smart as collies and didn't need any dog to tell them how to do their jobs. Lucia considered it an all-round win. Her team was productive and happy, and she could usually leave work early.

Before the announcement of the meeting on meetings, Lucia had been thinking about how she would love to leave early today. Another meeting, especially an afternoon one with a new boss, who would likely want to hear his own voice, would ruin her plans to get in some stick chasing before dinner. Lucia looked out her window, much more concerned with leaving early than with the fate of Barkers. After all, she was a well-educated engineer with years of experience. She could get a job anywhere, couldn't she?

"No, no," Charlie Chihuahua said when Stella called him. "No time. No time for meetings at all." Before Stella could use up any more of his time complaining about meetings on meetings, Charlie hung up.

Charlie Chihuahua, Head of Product Development, had been promoted for his on-the-job skills. Unfortunately, those skills didn't help him to manage others. Now, the only way he could make sure his department even came close to meeting its goals was to micromanage every project.

Charlie worked like a dog nearly every day of his life. He was always tired, always under pressure, and had no idea how to get the people he managed to do their jobs well enough so that he didn't have to help them. Unlike Lucia, Charlie never went home early, but his department performed no better than hers.

In her office, Stella harrumphed at the phone, annoyed Charlie hung up on her, and dialed Gary's number.

"I don't want to have this meeting," Gary howled when Stella told him why she was calling. "Minnie is happy about the meeting, but you know how she is. She doesn't see how terrible it will be. She never realizes how awful anything is. How can our new CEO call a meeting on his first day, especially when we all have deadlines to meet? I'm not ready. Not ready at all. Stella, what are we going to do?"

Can any dog be top dog?

"Don't worry, Gary," Stella said, pleased by his affirmation of her notions about Boxer. "I'll think of something. I'll email you with my ideas later."

Stella hung up the phone, now grinning a wolfish grin. One thing she wouldn't do, she knew, was call that meddling Minnie in K9 Resources. It was Stella's opinion that Minnie's job was an easy one and unessential to the smooth operation of Barkers. Any dog with the nose it was born with would have enough skill to take over K9 Resources. Even though she was Head of K9 Resources, Stella didn't think Minnie was much of a resource herself.

Stella hated knowing that Minnie was excitedly awaiting the meeting, no doubt looking forward to the opportunity to lick another CEO's muzzle in order to make herself look important. In fact, although she knew no one was supposed to have met the new CEO yet, Stella grew concerned that Minnie had secretly contacted him. This whole meeting on meetings was probably Minnie's idea, just so she could prance her paws in front of Mr. Bertie Boxer. For all Stella knew, Minnie already had her claws into Boxer. Stella couldn't decide what was going to be worse, listening to Boxer babble on or watching Minnie soak up his every word with those perky little pink and white ears.

Can't see
the bone for
the trees

Flexing her paws, Stella started typing an email to her fellow managers, detailing what she felt were the concerns they all shared about that afternoon's meeting on meetings. She was very thorough, leaving no detail out as she listed the facts, as she saw them. Stella even expounded at the end, using one or two of her favorite quotes, and urging the other managers, in the strongest terms possible, not to permit this frivolous disregard for their work time to prevail.

Dear Colleagues,

Thank you for sharing your thoughts on the Meeting on Meetings that we are all expected to attend this afternoon with the new CEO. I am confirming in this email the input I received from you all in my phone calls earlier today.

We all believe poor judgment was exercised in choosing the time of this meeting considering we all have serious deadlines to meet by the end of the month. We are also all at one in believing that it would have been a much better choice for the new CEO to meet each of us on a one on one basis.

I am confirming your input so that we can stand together at the meeting today and make the point to the new CEO that we are all very busy and cannot just drop everything to attend a meeting. I, for one, have a production schedule that has to be carefully managed. With the lower sales we are experiencing, and therefore shorter production runs, the line changeovers are more frequent and challenging to the overall efficiency of my manufacturing plant teams. After listening to all of you today, I understand you all share similar pressures.

This is what you told me:

- We already have too many meetings to attend
- We cannot change our work schedules at a

moment's notice
- The last CEOs didn't interfere with our day to day operations and left it up to the managers
- It would be more beneficial for the CEO to spend time learning our processes before he begins to bark
- We think the new CEO is getting off to a bad start with his managers by pitting us against one another regarding our processes
- We need to make a stand before everything gets changed for no good
- Did the Board lead Boxer to believe he could expect us to sit, beg and rollover at the snap of a finger?
- Is this the idea of the new CEO or another K9 Resources fur-brained plan?
- We will attend because we were told we have to, although none of us has the time
- The business will suffer with us away from our operations at this time

We need to decide who will be the spokesdog to bring this to the attention of Boxer.

I am copying all of you who spoke to me on this today. You will note, I have not copied K9 Resources, as I have a sneaking suspicion they are somehow behind this. Keep true to your word. Remember, you know more about Barkers than this new CEO and we are more valuable to this company than he is.

I will remind you of these famous quotes:

"Those dogs that don't like to burry bones themselves organize meetings. In the end, no one has time and no bones get buried."

– Thomas Howls

"It's the lazy dog who has the time to plan a meeting about it." – Wendell Woofler

In exasperation,
Stella Scottie
Manager Manufacturing and Plant Operations
Barkers Inc.

She reread her message several times, pleased at the stirring tone. Proud of herself, and sure her email would ruin all of Minnie's opportunities to show off in front of Boxer, Stella pressed send. Then she sat back, waiting for the affirmation to pour in.

Lucia opened the email in annoyance, hoping it wasn't more work for her to do, but when she read Stella's careful arguments and her quotes, Lucia's tail started to wag. Stella was right, another meeting was the last thing Barkers needed. How could any dog be expected to get their work done and go stick chasing if they were stuck in meetings all afternoon? This new boss sure thought highly of himself, calling together all of the managers and supervisors on his first day. This meeting was not going to be a good use of any dog's time.

The best thing to do, Lucia thought, was to forward the email to her friend Alex Affenpinscher in accounting, so they could share a good laugh about the new boss. Knowing how much time had been taken in selecting a new CEO for Barkers, Lucia thought it was a bit sad that the new boss seemed to be messing up already. Another waste of Barkers time.

Lucia, although very intelligent, didn't realize she was letting conjecture dictate where facts were scarce.

Charlie Chihuahua didn't have time to read Stella's email, but he could see it was important because it was very long, with bullet points. The thing to do, Charlie thought, was to forward it to every dog in his department. If the email concerned product development, the dogs he managed would storm his office like a pack of wolves, looking for help. He was sure to find out what was in the email then.

Tales wag faster than truths

Gary Golden read Stella's email, feeling nearly as much trepidation as when he'd read Boxer's. Gary didn't like emails with bullet points and confrontation. Gary liked each day to go smoothly, with a nice midday walk in the park, and no barking or biting. Even worse than a meeting where he had to justify his extra bones would be a meeting where there was a scuffle to see who was top dog. Gary put his paws over his eyes and whimpered.

It was going to be a terrible afternoon, Gary thought. A horrible afternoon. Boxer was sure to do some restructuring, which meant he would definitely let go of some of the staff. That was the only reason he would call in all the managers and supervisors at once, and on his first day.

Gary gnawed on that thought for so long he worked himself into a pant. Finally, he decided to call Minnie. As Head of K9 Resources, Minnie was sure to know if

Boxer would be able to let staff members go on his first day.

Don't run if your tail's on fire

"Fire us?" Minnie repeated when he barked out his concerns. "Gary, that's a dog-brained idea if I ever heard one. Does this have anything to do with the email every dog was talking about in accounting? Have you seen it?"

Gary admitted he had. He was already feeling calmer. Minnie's easy dismissal of his fears had Gary's tail almost wagging again.

"Could you forward it to me?" Minnie asked. "I'd like to read it and I won't ever say who forwarded it to me. Don't worry so much, Gary. Look at all the awards you've won in your time here. You're the best Head of Sales Barkers has ever had."

Minnie hung up and opened the email Gary forwarded to her, eager to see what all the barking was about. Her ears perked up in amusement as she read the outrageous bullet points and misappropriated quotes, but they flattened at the increasingly rabid string of replies attached.

Minnie was, in fact, an excellent judge of doggie nature and a top notch K9 Resources Manager. She knew that Stella's email was fuel to the fear many dogs had for their futures at Barkers. Minnie knew that fear was a powerful motivator, but one that took away a dog's ability to plan, reason and innovate. She was not fond of where Stella's email had her fellow Barkers employees headed. Some of them had obviously gone clear off their leashes.

> *A bone buried in panic will never be found*

Minnie didn't want to be a tattle-tale, but she knew it was her duty to warn Boxer of the trouble brewing at Barkers. Minnie had confidence that all the work which went into selecting Boxer for the job of CEO was good work. She also knew that Barkers was getting very near the brink of disaster. As K9 Resources Manager, she didn't like the idea of any dog, much less many dogs, losing their jobs. Since Minnie knew Boxer was the best hope they had of saving Barkers, she forwarded him the email.

Minnie's optimism was tested over the hours leading up to the meeting. She worried about what type of CEO Boxer would turn out to be. She worried about forwarding Stella's email and all the attached replies. Minnie was nervous for her colleagues, nervous for the future of Barkers and very nervous about the meeting. She even began to wish she hadn't worn her favorite bright bow, thinking that maybe she didn't want to attract attention after all.

Minnie didn't know it, but she was giving in to the overall atmosphere of fear and anxiety at Barkers. Naturally, every dog at Barkers had their share of concerns over the uncertainty of the company's future and the unknown quantity of the new CEO. That concern wouldn't have unraveled into this unrest, however, if not for Stella's rabblerousing.

Don't bark up the wrong tree

Though Stella hadn't realized it yet, she had made a number of mistakes that morning, and her greatest was judging the new CEO before meeting him. She got wrapped up in her own thoughts and feelings on the meeting on meetings, which caused her to hear only what she wanted to hear when she called her colleagues. Caught up in the sound of her own barking, she couldn't recognize how uncomfortable it was for her peers when she reveled in the power she felt and stirred up negative feedback.

Stella's second greatest mistake was the fatuous act of creating an email criticizing the first actions of the new CEO, and distributing it widely in a misguided attempt to undermine him. Foolishly, she seemed to have no concern her email would be forwarded, or of it being a topic for water bowl gossip.

Though her tactics were heavy-pawed and reckless, in one morning Stella had managed to create an unwelcome atmosphere of discontent and negativism in the ranks of the organization. Her actions, undoubtedly spurred by a need to feel important at Barkers, were inadvertently harming not only her standing, but the entire company. While professing to help, Stella was in fact creating a dangerous situation for every dog, especially herself.

The sled won't budge if we all pull in different directions

At the appointed time that afternoon, after long lunches spent bolstering each other's fears with conjecture and gossip, all of the managers and supervisors filed down the hall toward the conference room. They had their tails down and their ears drooped with worry. Gary, every dog could hear, was even whimpering, the calm Minnie had given him ruined by a lunchtime talk with Stella.

Stella Scottie walked down the hall with a smug look on her naturally long face. Her lips were curled in a grin, because of all the support she imagined she had from the other managers. Her stubby tail pointed straight up. She huffed, blowing air through her well-groomed mustache, and marched forward, ready for battle.

Minnie Westie observed all this with dismay. She expected Stella would confront Boxer before their new CEO could even open the meeting. If that didn't happen, Minnie was worried Stella would interrupt and undermine Boxer at every turn. This would undercut the hierarchy of Barkers and be the ruin of them all. Now it was Minnie's turn to whine, drawing a look of concern from Gary.

Scuttling on her short legs, Stella trotted right past the other dogs, who were all but slinking down the hallway, and barreled into the conference room. Stella was ready to sink her teeth into this Boxer from Britain, but what she saw in the conference room gave her pause.

A barking
dog never
bites

In the middle of the large room, where there was usually a long conference table with chairs, stood Boxer, surrounded by a wide circle of tripods. Each tripod had markers and an oversized flip chart of paper. Stella had no idea what to make of such an arrangement. Meetings were always conducted sitting around the table, where it was easy to let your mind wander to more important things, like how boring the meeting was, how much work you could be getting done if you weren't in it, and wondering when it would end.

"Come in, come in," Boxer said, looking quite cheerful.

As Stella entered, the other managers and the supervisors trailing her, she noticed Bertie Boxer had on a very nice red tie. Not knowing where else to go or what else to do, Stella led the others into the circle of flip charts.

"It's nice to finally meet you all," Bertie Boxer said, and Stella had the strange feeling he was saying it right to her.

Bertie went on to introduce himself, asking each of them, in turn, to introduce themselves to him. Knowing it was important to get to the heart of things quickly, Bertie spent just five minutes giving an overview of his previous positions. All the managers and supervisors were a little surprised at the diverse range of experiences Boxer had with other international companies. Boxer concluded that, in the next few days, he intended to schedule one-on-one events with every manager and supervisor, to get know them and vice versa. "But right now, we're going to have a different type of meeting," Boxer said. "I have, as you see, removed the table and chairs. They aren't gone forever, but today I want to make sure every dog participates equally."

Gary shrank a bit at this, but Minnie's tail began to wag. She liked Boxer's tone, which was sure but friendly and, so far, devoid of censure.

"The board tells me there are complaints, from suppliers, retailers and customers alike, that it's impossible to contact any dog at Barkers because every dog is always in a meeting," Boxer said. "From the board's description of the way things are done here at Barkers, it sounds as if the meeting culture has grown out of control. I'd like to find out if that's true. Together, we're going to investigate how decisions are made at Barkers."

Boxer looked around the room, almost as if daring any dog to interrupt him. "Now, I would like to commence the Meeting on Meetings," he said. "A subject which, I gather, has caused some unrest this morning."

Every dog waited for Stella to burst forward with a prepared speech on why this was a bad idea. She tried to rally her thoughts, derailed by Boxer's calm demeanor and straightforward words, but her carefully prepared phrases ran away like chipmunks. She looked around for support, and was greeted by silence as her fellow managers and the supervisors all looked away.

"If there are no questions," Bertie Boxer said, "I would like you each to select a flip chart. There's one for everyone."

He then turned back the cover to the first page of his flip chart, which he'd prepared in advance. "This is my planned weekly Leadership Team Meeting," he said, standing to the side so they could all see. "We're going to examine it together, looking at who will attend, what is accomplished, and how much it costs Barkers for us to hold it."

"As you can see," Bertie Boxer said, "This is the title, Leadership Team Meeting. I am the chairman of the meeting, and the managers are listed as attendees." He went on to point out the frequency of the meeting, the duration, and what important decisions were to be made. The final line, the approximate cost of the meeting, Bertie had underlined in red. "The cost of the meeting is the number of managers attending multiplied by the number of hours the meeting takes up and an approximate hourly salary rate." Bertie made eye contact with each of them, making sure he still had their attention.

All around the room, the managers and supervisors nodded. Bertie's chart made sense and was easy to follow. They could picture making charts like this for their own meetings.

CEO Leadership Team Meeting

Chair: Bertie Boxer

Attendees: Gary Golden, Minnie Westie, Stella Scottie, Charlie Chihuahua, Lucia Lowchen, Berlinda Basset, Lorenzo Labrador

Frequency: Weekly

Duration: 3 hours

Decisions Made: Direction for senior managers to act on

Approximate Cost: $10,000

That, of course, was exactly what Bertie wanted them to do. "On your flip chart paper," he said, "Using my Leadership Team Meeting as the example, I'd like you to document all the important meetings you hold each week or month. You can get started now."

With such a clear example to guide them, and Bertie looking on with a smile, the managers and supervisors of Barkers found it easy to complete the request. Some of them, like Minnie, even found it fun.

Others, like Gary, found it educational. Gary had no idea all of his meetings were costing so much money. He couldn't help but think about how much it would help

Barkers to keep that money, especially when he could see the meetings weren't really accomplishing very much. Gary was starting to realize that organizing all of his meetings wasn't really him doing his job effectively. Rather, going to all of his meetings was taking up time he and his team could be using to do the real job of making sales. Gary thought about the last time he received a special bonus for outstanding sales achievements, and realized it was a long time ago. He wondered if he could get back to achieving more in the future, if he didn't waste so much time in meetings.

Stella stared at her flip chart paper, wishing she could think of something wrong with Bertie Boxer's request, but she couldn't. In fact, his idea was so simple and his example so easy to follow, she found herself writing about her own meetings almost before she knew it. As she wrote out page after page, Stella was pleased to see what she already knew, what she had been saying all day. She wasted too much time going to meetings. She had to grudgingly admit, it was nice to have such concrete evidence of her complaint. Stella, in fact, felt vindicated.

When Bertie observed the writing had stopped, as all the meetings had been recorded, he called the managers and supervisors to the center of the room. "I'd like each of you, in turn, to tell the group all about the meetings you chair, who attends, and so on," he said. "Stella, we'll start with you. What's your first meeting?"

Stella, who had grown quite enthusiastic about showing how right she was when she said Barkers had too many meetings, was happy to go first. She was also sure that going first was a reward. Stella knew Bertie had watched her the most while every dog was working on the flip charts. He obviously saw what an exemplary job she was doing on her charts and decided she should go first as an example to the rest of the pack.

Smugness is not good grooming

Stella Scottie went through each meeting she chaired. Prompted by questions from Bertie Boxer and the others, she explained to her fellow managers, and the supervisors, who attended her meetings and what was decided. She took particular pleasure in detailing how much of her time the meetings took up, how much they cost Barkers, and how often dogs who were needed at the meetings didn't even show up.

This last point of Stella's caused some grumbling and growling, expressions of discontent which only grew in volume. Many of the dogs, it seemed, felt that they were asked to attend too many meetings. Yet, the same dogs were disgruntled by the inconsistent attendance at the meetings they held. Others, including Gary, seemed to show up at almost every meeting, even if they didn't really need to be there. Another problem, one Bertie noticed quite keenly, was that top dogs were sending other dogs in their place, but those dogs didn't have the authority to make any decisions or, in some cases, even know enough to supply useful information and be part of the decision process.

"I don't have time to attend your Sales Planning Meeting," Charlie Chihuahua snipped at Gary. "I'm already attending Stella's Production Sales Forecast Meeting and Lucia's Sales Forecast Meeting. Why do we have so many sales meetings, anyway?"

"Why aren't I invited to your Sales Forecast Meeting?" Gary howled at Lucia. "I'm Head of Sales, remember."

"I invited you once," Lucia sniffed. "You didn't show up. You were probably out chasing golf balls."

"I chase golf balls?" Gary snarled. "You're the one who is always wasting time gnawing on all the free bones those engineering sales reps bring you."

"Go chase a stick off a bridge, Gary," Alex Affenpinscher said, defending his friend Lucia.

Barking dogs can't hear

"Hold on," said Bertie, sensing they were getting a bit far afield.

The dogs ignored him, continuing to yip about whose meetings were really important, who should attend them and who should not. Bertie frowned, adjusted his favorite red tie, and took a deep breath.

"I say," Bertie barked firmly. "That's enough of that. Arguing in this way is not my style of how to get agreement at a meeting."

Bertie didn't use a loud bark, or an angry bark, but the censure in his tone brought the others up short. Heads turned toward Bertie and tails stopped thumping in anger. Every dog felt a little ashamed, realizing they were acting like a pack of hyenas in front of their new CEO.

"From what I can see," Bertie began, feeling no need to alienate them with further reprimands now that he'd curtailed their arguing, "we have a Sales Planning Meeting, a Sales Forecast Meeting, a Short Term Sales Forecast Meeting, a Long Term Sales Forecast Meeting and a Production Sales Forecast Meeting."

All around Bertie Boxer the other dogs nodded. When Bertie listed all the various sales meetings in the company, they began to realize it was really very silly. Stella started to think that maybe she didn't need a Production Sales Forecast Meeting if she could attend or combine with one of the other meetings on sales. Lucia considered that maybe her Sales Forecast Meeting could be combined with Gary's Sales Planning Meeting.

Do I sense a paws?

Now that he had them back on track, Bertie helped the team complete the task of reviewing each of the

Leadership Teams' individual meetings. As they went over each meeting, all the managers and supervisors began to realize that many of the meetings they were holding were forums about similar business issues, and a duplication of effort. Having so many meetings about similar business areas, often without the right dogs even present, was a waste of every dog's time and Barkers' resources. Even Stella had to admit to herself, this meeting on meetings wasn't frivolous after all. What was frivolous was the high number of other meetings currently being held at Barkers.

By the time the meeting on meetings was over, a number of meetings had been eliminated. Equally important, every manager and supervisor dog came to an agreement about who should attend each of the meetings. Bertie made it very clear that only dogs who could make decisions for their department and could provide information relevant to the meeting topic should attend. More than that, if a dog was unable to attend an agreed upon meeting, they were asked to notify the meeting chair at least a day in advance and to provide an agreed upon substitute. Barking over a conference call phone line was discouraged and not the best option for these key meetings.

Bertie Boxer then requested the creation and publication of an efficient meeting calendar for use by all managers and supervisors and for it to be visible to all members of the company. The calendar would detail the location and duration of each meeting, as well as who should attend. Bertie knew, and the others could see, that every dog would benefit from the right dogs attending the meetings. Clear decisions could be made, concrete actions taken, and time and money saved. Minnie Westie, her optimism restored and vindicated, spearheaded the creation and publication of the Barkers meeting calendar.

Happy as a dog

Minnie wasn't the only one now feeling more optimistic about the future of Barkers. After the meeting on meetings, Lucia Lowchen stopped spending so much of her time staring out the window dreaming about chasing sticks. Even though the new meeting schedule allowed her to use her time more efficiently, she didn't go home early anymore. Lucia, in fact, found her work ethic refueled by the new management style of Bertie Boxer. Moreover, the enthusiasm she'd all but forgotten she once had for her job was now reinvigorated.

Charlie Chihuahua, always a bit highly-strung, still worked like a dog every day, but now he was working at managing his department, instead of micromanaging it. Charlie found that Bertie Boxer was an excellent CEO and that Charlie, always an intelligent Chihuahua, could learn how to manage his department better by mimicking Bertie's encouraging management style. Charlie even found that, as Bertie was always encouraging, he could go to his new CEO and discuss product issues, and seek advice, instead of working overtime to try and solve the issues alone. Charlie now looked forward to fewer meetings, where he could show off his newfound confidence and his department's performance.

A shaggy dog story

Gary the Golden was, at first, quite sad about the outcome of the meeting on meetings. He no longer got to spend his time traveling around, meeting other dogs in fun, interesting and usually food filled places. Instead, he had to work out of the central office, from where he coordinated local representation in all the places he used go. To Gary's relief, however, he didn't lose any of his precious bones, as he once feared.

To the surprise of many, Gary soon came to appreciate his new role. He realized that he could do his job much better when he wasn't constantly driving and flying. He also had more time to spend with his little Goldens, something he hadn't even realized he wanted to do until he was given the chance. Gary became happier, leaner, and eventually qualified for a performance bonus, something he hadn't enjoyed in a long time.

Even Stella was happy with the outcome of the meeting on meetings. She did, of course, have to endure quite a bit of ribbing for what seemed like dog-years afterwards. Her fellow managers didn't quickly forget how much trouble she stirred up before the meeting, or how, once they were at the meeting, Stella dove wholeheartedly into Bertie Boxer's plan, not even mumbling a word about the email and her rabblerousing actions. Stella eventually regained her Scottie strut, although it took a little time.

Interestingly, Stella was increasingly pleased with how much more efficient Barkers became under Bertie Boxer. She felt he took a keen interest in her Manufacturing and Plant Operations and was supportive. Of all the recent CEOs, Stella was beginning to believe that Bertie was the one to lead Barkers out of its recent slump and on to greater things. In particular, Stella was pleased at how no one, not even Bertie, was allowed to miss a meeting she chaired. At least, not if they were supposed to attend.

Part Two: The Reality

Meetings – All Shapes and Sizes

Good meetings don't just happen . . .

There are effective (positive) meetings and ineffective (negative) meetings. The positive meetings leave attendees energized and ready to accomplish the next task. A negative meeting leaves participants wondering why they showed up to waste so much of their time.

THE KEY TO EFFECTIVE MEETINGS IS THE MEETING LEADER
A good leader has the skills to organize a meeting where he or she has the ability to encourage other attendees to participate and be an active part of the process, which results in a positive outcome.

Effective meetings have three major outcomes:
- The goals of the meeting are achieved
- The attendees believe in the meeting process and outcomes
- The time taken to achieve the result was justified

Can meetings be avoided altogether?
Although most businesses would like to avoid meetings altogether, it's not possible to avoid them completely. Even smaller businesses cannot avoid them.

What are common key mistakes?
- For good meetings to take place, we must avoid a number of pitfalls, such as:

• Open ended discussions without an agenda
• Unrealistic expectations of how the meeting will be managed
• Time wasting at meetings

Different types of meetings - One simple rule

There are many different types of meetings that take place within large and small companies, such as action-oriented meetings, short term planning meetings, long term planning meetings and even 'brain storming' meetings.

One common thread will make all of these different meetings effective: making sure the planning for the event is done in advance. This will ensure there is always a reason or purpose for the meeting.

Take the Right Steps – Plan Your Meeting

Issue an agenda

The invited members of the meeting need to know, in advance, the purpose of the meeting and an agenda needs to be issued. It's best if a time is allocated for each item to be discussed so that it's clear for everyone 'what and for how long.' That is, what each agenda item is and for how long it will be debated.

Are the right people invited?

It is most important to make sure the right people are invited to the meeting and crucial that all areas of the company impacted by the decisions being made are invited to be present. However, don't allow any one area of the company to be overrepresented, as that can inappropriately influence the discussions.

Meeting location

One area of how to run effective meetings that is often overlooked is the actual meeting room or location. A location that is central and easy to get to for all attendees is a bonus and will make sure you get the people you need there for discussion and decision making. The meeting room layout is also important. A round table, for example, is always an advantage, if the meeting size can accommodate it. All attendees can see each other and it encourages a contribution from every individual present. If a classroom layout is selected, it usually sends a message to the attendees, when they arrive, that they are going to be lectured to at this meeting. The last aspect of location to consider is incorporating the tools necessary for conducting the meeting. For example, if people will need to write, make sure you have pens, paper, flip charts and working markers for use at the meeting.

Conference calls

The conference call is one of the most disliked aspects of office life, but it does save travel expense and can be useful if managed correctly. When using conference calls, meeting leaders need to set appropriate basic rules, complete and unambiguous, which are different from the rules for face-to-face meetings, and employ tighter and more explicit agendas. Leaders need to work harder to get attendees participating and talking, both by asking questions and by listening more. The agendas and goals of the meeting should be made very clear, and even more explicit than for face-to-face meetings, to avoid people's attention being distracted. The number of people dialing in should be kept to a minimum to avoid loss of focus.

Start and finish on time

Time management is also an important element of running an effective meeting. Start your meeting on time, even if some attendees have not arrived. Build a reputation for this and you will find that your invited team members will make a big effort to be early at your meetings, in the future. Also, try to finish on time, as some of your attendees will have other events in their calendar and will have to leave at the expected meeting finish time. Members leaving before the meeting ends can disrupt the discussion and spoil the meeting.

How long is a meeting?

This can depend on the scope of the meeting and the size of the group in the discussion. However, most effective meetings last for less than three hours. This is because, though it can vary, most meeting attendees maintain concentration, at a high level of involvement, for a maximum of three hours. Attendees should never be asked to sit for more than 1½ hours at a time.

What if an agenda item runs over?

During the meeting, it is inevitable that some agenda items will go over the time limits. The meeting leader will have to decide, on a 'subject by subject' basis, whether it is acceptable or the discussion should be held over for another meeting.

Concluding - Confirm the decisions and who will take action

At the conclusion of discussion on each agenda item, good meeting leaders confirm to the meeting attendees the decisions and actions agreed upon, and will detail who is taking action, together with a timeline for implementation. These decisions and actions should be confirmed in brief written minutes.

Troubleshooting Your Meeting - Is it Working?

If you hear any of these comments in one of your meeting, it's not going well:
- What time is this meeting due to start?
- What's the added value here?
- What's the objective of this meeting?
- This is too much data to comprehend
- Is she asleep?
- We're rambling
- Is this on the agenda?
- That's bad behavior
- Let someone else speak, you're dominating the meeting
- Some of us seem to be disengaged because of laptops and phones
- Are we going to have a break?
- What did we decide?
- Can we move on?
- That's not how we did it at . . .
- They came late and now they're leaving early
- We're talking over people
- You're talking at us, not with us

What can you do?
If you do hear one of the above comments at one of your meetings, or ones similar to them, go back over the key steps listed earlier and try to see where your meeting went astray. Did you invite the right people? Were an appropriate time and location selected? Was the meeting room ready? Did you issue a detailed and realistic agenda?

An honest reevaluation of your meeting after the fact, in view of the suggested format above, should reveal where your meeting could have been improved. Don't be discouraged by a less than optimal meeting. It is likely that you're potentially working against years of poor meeting habits in your company or organization. The more you work toward managing good meetings, the more efficient your meetings will become and you can expect better results to follow. Also, others will see the value of an on-time and productive meeting, and they will become better attendees as well.

A Real Life Example - How Does the Author Manage His Meetings as a CEO?

Weekly meetings
My weekly Leadership Team Meeting would be scheduled for every Monday at 14:00. This allowed all the senior managers to prepare for the meeting, have face-desk time with their departmental staff in advance of the meeting, and to be current with the business.

Agenda published three days in advance
An agenda was published three days in advance, with time allocated for each subject. Any manager could propose an agenda item for the meeting.

Same time, same place
I tried to make sure the Monday meeting took place every week at the same time, as I expected all senior managers to be present or agree with me in advance for a substitute to attend. Any substitute had to have the authority to act for his or her manager.

Meeting room checked in advance
The meeting room was checked just prior to the meeting to ensure flip charts were available, the markers actually work, computer connections were up and running and the room clean and tidy. Refreshments were included prior to the meeting start time.

Meeting started on time
The meetings started on time. Even if all managers were not yet present.

Agenda item 1: What's on your mind?

This is a concept I borrowed from a former boss at General Motors, Darwin Clark. All managers were encouraged to bring up a topic which was on their worry list, and important enough that it could have an impact on the company performance or could have an impact on the other team members. It was understood and guaranteed that the subject would be discussed at the end of the published agenda and before the meeting was closed. The subject was listed on a flip chart for all to see. Everybody knew it would be covered during the meeting on that day.

Agenda item 2: Actions follow up
Second on the agenda was always a review of the actions from any previous Leadership Team Meetings, if the completion date of the task fell within the window of that week's meeting.

Agenda with time allocation
The other agenda items would then be listed, together with an allocation of time for each discussion. At the end of the published agenda, the 'What's on your mind?' subject would be brought to the table for discussion, and actions agreed upon. Sometimes, there were multiple WOYM items.

List actions and responsible person(s)
Before the meeting closed, the list of actions, and those responsible for the actions, would be displayed to the team.

Distribute meeting minutes and action points
Within 24 hours of the meeting, brief minutes and the action points would be circulated to all Leadership Team members.

Feedback

Feedback was solicited from team members on how the meeting process was working and adjustments were made.

Conclusion

Managing a meeting can be fun

Right from the start, to have a positive energy in the meeting, set an example and display energy and engagement. Do this right from when the meeting attendees arrive. Very quickly, the meeting will reflect your mood and energy level. If there is a positive and energetic atmosphere, the meeting will be positive and energetic.

When opening the meeting, it goes a long way to setting the mood and tone of the meeting when a few words are said about why everyone is together and what the expected outcome of the meeting is. Introducing a little appropriate humor also helps keep a positive atmosphere throughout the meeting. Also, try putting just as much energy into closing the meeting as preparing the opening remarks.

Whatever you do, don't be discouraged. Developing good meeting skills and encouraging a positive meeting culture takes time.

I have attended very few perfect meetings . . .
I have witnessed many dull and boring ones . . .

This process is the cure!

Book Two

BARKERS ON SAVINGS

INTRODUCTION

On a visit to Japan, I can remember the Chairman of Suzuki telling me, 'top down,' cost down, and 'bottom up,' cost up. In other words, if you leave the process of budgeting to employee teams building from zero, the end result will be a cost increase. I do not agree with this philosophy, and prefer to rely on a winning process which makes savings a task set up to involve the total organization, with everyone pulling together for a common goal.

One type of business especially at risk for this behavior is newer businesses where the founder still takes a strong day to day role in the running of the company. In the early days of a company, the entrepreneur has to make all of the decisions and do all of the daily work. Difficulties can ensue when the founder has trouble trusting the employees hired later. At a certain point, the company originator needs to loosen the reigns and let the new, qualified staff perform the tasks they were hired for before they become dissatisfied and the best people depart.

If the maximum opportunity for savings is to be realized, savings in any company should not rely on just a 'top down' or a 'bottom up' approach but rather a combination of the two. The best way I've found to do this, a tried and tested way, can be found below. First, enjoy seeing how Bertie Boxer will accomplish savings.

PART ONE: THE STORY

In the center of the city of St. Bernard, deep in the heart of the Midwestern United States, stood a monument to mid-nineteenth century corporate style architecture, with a noticeable baroque influence. This grand old building was the headquarters of Barkers, Inc., an international canine accessories company. The manufacturing and distribution areas of Barkers had long since outgrown this original building. It now held cubicles and meeting rooms, copy machines and water coolers, and everything else the managerial staff of Barkers needed. It also held an office, magnificently devoid of alterations to its original baroque style, where Bertie Boxer paced.

Bertie Boxer, the new CEO of Barkers, Inc., stopped in front of the fireplace, which no longer functioned, and looked in the mirror hanging above it. He adjusted his favorite red tie. "We need to sniff out savings and cut commercial expenses," he said to his reflection, rehearsing for the meeting he was about to call. "Our profits are deteriorating and we need to save costs to compensate. At the same time, we need to generate more revenue."

Bertie nodded to himself. It sounded reasonable. It sounded correct. He knew what every dog would really hear, though. They would hear, "The new boss from Britain wants to take away my job." Bertie couldn't have them hearing that, especially since he didn't want to take away their jobs at all. Bertie knew that a dog afraid of losing his bones was a dog who wasn't thinking well. If he was going to find a way to save money and keep their jobs, he needed them to be thinking well so they could help support the goals.

As was his habit, Bertie wrote himself a note and stuck it to the mirror.

A worried dog can't find any bones

The first thing to do, of course, was to announce the meeting. Bertie returned to his desk and opened his email. He created an address list that included everyone at Barkers, from Sales to Shipping and from Accounts to Acquisitions. For Bertie's savings plan to work, every dog at Barkers must be included.

Dear Barkers' Employees,

I would like every dog to join me in the main warehouse, area A, on Wednesday the 1st at 3:00 PM for a companywide meeting. Every dog at Barkers, Inc. is asked to attend this All Employee Meeting, with no exceptions. The meeting will begin promptly at 3:00 PM.

This will be an opportunity for me, your new

C.E.O., to introduce myself to every dog at Barkers. Following my introduction, the first ever All Employee Meeting will commence. This meeting will bring together all employees to directly address a key issue at Barkers, Inc. and, therefore, involves every dog in every department. No preparations are necessary for this meeting. Please do not bring your computers, phones or papers to the conference room.

Sincerely,
Bertie Boxer
Chief Executive Officer
Barkers Inc.

When Bertie was done composing his email, he read it over three times to ensure it was correct. Taking a deep breath, he hit send. Bertie knew that once an email left your outbox, you couldn't take it back. He also knew that, no matter how carefully he worded it, every dog who read it would interpret something different from what it said. That was the nature of emails, and why Bertie preferred to speak to others muzzle to muzzle, but it wouldn't be a good use of his time to personally invite everyone to the meeting.

News of Bertie Boxer's meeting spread quickly through Barkers, and Bertie wouldn't have been surprised by the reactions it sparked in his fellow employees. Minnie Westie, the head of K9 Resources, read the email with tail-wagging enthusiasm. What a great idea, she thought, to include every dog on such an important issue, because savings affected them all. Gary Golden, Head of Sales, stifled his initial reaction of worry, reminding himself how well Boxer's other actions had played out for Barkers. Stella Scottie,

Manager of Manufacturing and Plant Operations and a onetime critic of Boxer, nodded sagely. If Bertie Boxer wanted a company-wide meeting, she was certain it was a good idea. In fact, if she heard any dog saying it wasn't, she would set them straight, just see if she wouldn't.

> *Overzealous watchdogs might bight the wrong hand*

Where Boxer's email didn't meet with acceptance and enthusiasm, however, was with the Warehouse and Distribution Team. Team members gathered on their lunch break, every tongue wagging about Boxer's planned meeting. Among the loudest was Arthur Afghan, a lean old hound who had worked for Barkers for nearly thirty years.

"A company-wide meeting to take place in our warehouse, of all things," Arthur barked. "They'll probably want us to set up a stage for the top dogs to parade around on. As if we have nothing else to do but set things up and take down things for them. We'll do all that work just so we can waste the afternoon watching their version of best in show."

"They don't know what real work is," Priya Pekingese said. "They eat five lunches a day, schmoosing dogs from other companies, at all the best chow halls in St. Bernard. It's all on Barkers' dime, and you can bet your tail they won't give any of that up. That's not where the savings will come."

"That's right," Arthur barked. "And what do we get? No fancy chow for us. At best, they hand out free collars with the company logo on them every now and then."

"They could save money on those," Waseem Weimaraner said. "No one ever wears company collars at home."

"What about all that traveling they do?" Priya said, happy to gnaw on one of her favorite topics. "Running here and there, when a phone call would suffice, while we can't even get enough dogs on our team to do our jobs."

"Actually," Waseem said, "I heard the new boss already cut back on lunches and travel."

"We're the ones who do the real work at Barkers," Arthur said, ignoring Waseem's attempt to be reasonable. "Who makes sure the customers have what they paid for? That's what makes the money. That's what funds those chowhounds in their fancy office building downtown."

"And what about this shutdown time?" Priya snarled. "All departments are to shut down for three hours for this meeting? How can our schedule accommodate that? Ever since they added the new lines last year, we can't keep up, let alone deal with shutdown time. It just goes to show how out of touch management is with what goes on out here."

"I'll tell you what we should do," Arthur said, lowering his voice to a conspiratorial woof. "We should tell this new boss Boxer all about it, when he has his meeting here. We'll tell him in front of the whole company, so they can't ignore us, not this time."

Arthur nodded at his own declaration, his long ears bobbing. Waseem's brow wrinkled as he contemplated the prospect and Priya's face creased in a Pekingese smile. Putting their noses together, the three began discussing just how they would carry out Arthur's plan.

> *Plans and plots are only dog ears apart*

    Little did the dogs on the Warehouse and Distribution Team know, similar barking was being unleashed all over the company. In accounting, Alex Affenphinscher was woofing away over his lunch, expounding on how numbers didn't lie. In customer relations, dogs barked about the real work they did, of handling the all-important customers. They had to bark bark bark on the phones all day, sometimes to very irate consumers, while management were a bunch of lazy dogs in cushy offices.

    All over Barkers, tongues wagged, no dog getting any work done while they snipped about how they did the real work. Few dogs stopped to contemplate the good that could come of Bertie's meeting, or the reasoning behind it. It seemed to them, this meeting was the perfect opportunity to air long held grievances and finally make the rest of Barkers aware of how much credit they deserved. It didn't occur to them that, in view of the financial straits Barkers faced, there couldn't be much credit to go around.

    On the day of the All Employee Meeting, the first ever held at Barkers, Bertie Boxer went to the warehouse early to make sure his careful preparations were in place. He was pleased to see that space had been cleared for the meeting and the seating he requested brought in. Bertie tested several of the seats to make sure everyone would be able to see the large screen he had setup for his presentation. Satisfied, he moved to his spot in front of the screen to make sure everything was ready there as well. Bertie knew that proper preparation was half of any successful meeting.

Let
well-prepared
tails wag

Soon, other dogs started arriving. Bertie smiled to see many of them shaking paws and introducing themselves. Bertie knew that, although he had higher expectations for the meeting, just giving the dogs at Barkers this chance to meet each other was already an important accomplishment. After all, how could a company have good interdepartmental communication if dogs didn't even know one another?

Once it appeared that every dog had arrived, with a punctuality that pleased Bertie, he stepped in front of the screen, gathering their attention, and began his meeting. "Good afternoon," said Bertie, who liked to start meetings off on a pleasant note. "Thank you all for making room in your schedules for this first ever All Employee Meeting. We have a lot to cover today, and I hope we make some real progress and achieve some results. First, let me tell you a bit about who I am."

Bertie, who had already met all of the management at Barkers, as well as many other staff members, felt it was important to give a brief overview of his history and credentials. He wasn't selling himself to the dogs of Barkers, but he wanted them to know he had the experience to understand their daily tasks, accomplishments and concerns. He also hoped knowing more about him would help the other dogs find him approachable. A good manager had time for every employee; a great manager could tell which ones deserved more of it. One of Bertie's skills was properly assessing which dogs should be given time to express good, helpful thoughts, and which dogs only wanted attention and to hear the sound of their own bark.

Following his brief introduction, Bertie launched into an overview of the company's performance. "As you can see," Bertie said, pointing to the large graphs and tables on the screen behind him. "Our costs keep going up, while our revenue is trending down. Every dog knows that leads to a decrease in our profits. If the situation becomes much worse, Barkers will be in the doghouse."

"The two sides to this, money coming in and money going out, need to be addressed separately, of course. For the duration of this meeting, please set aside thoughts on our decreased revenue for another time. Today, I've gathered every dog together to address ways in which Barkers can reduce costs and save money."

All around the warehouse, full to the lip with dogs of all shapes, coats and sizes, eyes were fixed on Bertie, waiting for his next words. He knew this was an important moment in his plan, which he hoped would include all of Barkers. All the dogs were aware of the company's falling profits. What they really wanted to know, and were waiting to hear, was what their new boss Bertie Boxer intended to do about it, and what he wanted from them.

There's no such thing as a free bone

Mostly, every dog waited to hear if their job was safe. As Bertie knew, dogs worried about being let go could only think of their own jobs. He needed every dog to think about Barkers and how it ran, not how many bones they had saved for a rainy day. If Barkers was to come out of this tailspin, they needed all paws on deck.

Arthur Afghan, Priya Pekingese and Waseem Weimaraner exchanged smug grins, sensing their chance to start barking was near. Little did they know, Alex Affenphinscher and his accounting team had similar plans, as did the hounds in Customer Relations. What none of them knew was that Bertie Boxer, well versed in doggie nature, was prepared for a little barking, snipping and snarling. For, while he might be amiable and wear a stylish bow tie, Bertie was still a boxer.

"Every dog here is part of the solution to fencing in our increased spending," Bertie said. "I'm convinced there isn't a single dog at Barkers who doesn't have a good idea or three buried somewhere. The best thing to do is to dig them up."

Many dogs nodded, Stella Scottie with the most enthusiasm, as Stella was always sure of herself in her indomitable Scottie way. Of course they had good ideas, and every dog liked to dig. Why, telling their new boss their cost saving ideas would be even more

79

satisfying than barking about them around the water bowl on break.

"Every savings idea is a good idea," Bertie Boxer said. "We need to hear them all. In fact, I would like each of you to think of your top three, toy sized or giant. Every idea will get its time in the show ring, and every idea will have a champion to see it through." Bertie knew that even the best ideas wouldn't work without some dog being responsible for them. Ideas didn't have paws of their own. Someone had to walk them.

> *Time in the ring breeds confidence*

Bertie went on to give them his three ideas, none of which, to every dogs' relief, included cuts to salaries or jobs. He said he'd spotted unread magazines and newspapers littering the reception and break areas. Those subscriptions could be canceled. Then, to Gary Golden's sorrow, Bertie requested that snacks no longer be ordered for meetings which customers weren't attending.

What pleased Minnie Westie most was Bertie's suggestion that they not go outside the company for services when the talent they needed was at Barkers already. Minnie, as head of K9 Resources, liked to encourage every dog at Barkers to contribute to their full potential. She liked the idea so much, she began working out a plan to request a list of special skills from every dog, so she would know whom to call on when needed.

Seeing other dogs nodding, ears perked up, Arthur Afghan started to feel his opportunity to set matters straight about how neglected Warehouse and Distribution was slipping away. If he, Priya and Waseem didn't take this chance to let every dog know their complaints, when would they get another? Every dog would leave the meeting happy and thinking Barkers was on the way back up, and Arthur wouldn't stand for that.

So he did stand, nudging Priya Pekingese and Waseem Weimaraner, who sat to each side of him, to stand as well. Bertie Boxer stopped speaking and every dog turned to look at them. Arthur growled a little, his hackles up.

A bone missed is a bone lost

"This is all fine," Arthur said, "But how can we worry about savings when our department is broken?"

"What department is that?" Bertie Boxer asked, his tone polite. "Please provide your names and department, so all the dogs here know who is speaking."

Encouraged by Bertie's courteous response, Arthur stood up taller, is long ears bobbing. "I'm Arthur Afghan, and these are Priya Pekingese and Waseem Weimaraner. We're on the Warehouse and Distribution Team, and we don't have time to look for savings. We don't even have time for this meeting. We aren't top dogs, with nothing better to do."

"We don't even have enough dogs on hand to work our jobs," Priya Pekingese barked. "Ever since the new product lines were introduced eighteen months ago, we're always behind. Customer Relations is always yapping at us, but what can we do? We're working as hard as we can."

"And do you think we can get any dog in management to care?" Arthur Afghan woofed. "They sit in their offices, slapping bad reviews on our department, ruining our chances for bonus bones, but have they tried fixing things? When the new lines opened, they asked what we needed and we told them, but we never got it. They just stay away, as if ignoring our problems will bury them under a bush. Before this meeting, no one in the warehouse had seen a dog from management in a year."

Other members of the Warehouse and Distribution Team were standing now, too, and barking was starting to fill the air. Tails swished and ears swiveled. Alex Affenphinscher stood up, not wanting to miss a chance to dig up his grievances. Garry Golden sunk low in his seat, because there was nothing Gary liked less than angry yapping. Stella Scottie stood up, preparing to tell all the other dogs to sit down.

Don't yap so loudly that you can't hear

"Hold on," Bertie said, before the situation could fly off the leash. He respected every dog's right to voice their concerns, and fixing the Warehouse and

Distribution Team's problems seemed like the sort of thing that could, ultimately, lead to savings, but this was not how Bertie Boxer conducted meetings. "I said, hold on a moment," he repeated, louder.

Every dog fell silent, their tails stilling. Prick-eared dogs swiveled their ears toward Bertie, the scent hounds turned their noses his way, and the sight hounds tracked him with intent, bright eyes. Bertie nodded to the Warehouse and Distribution Team, who all quickly sat down. Soon, only Alex Affenphinscher was still standing, but no one noticed, as Affenphinschers were quite low to the ground.

"Thank you, Mr. Afghan, and the rest of the Warehouse and Distribution Team, for bringing this issue to my attention," Bertie said. "I know it isn't easy to stand up in front of all these dogs, many of whom you don't even know, and speak out. I appreciate that you value Barkers and your department enough to show such bravery."

Around the warehouse, Bertie could see dogs relaxing. He knew they had been worried he would be angry, but it took much more than a little barking to ruffle Bertie Boxer's fur. Looking back to Arthur Afghan, Bertie continued. "However, I'm afraid the issue of the new product lines isn't a subject for this meeting. This is a companywide meeting addressing savings."

Keep your eye on the blue ribbon

Bertie could see Afghan's jowls droop in a frown. "As important an issue as the Warehouse and Distribution Team's concern about properly accommodating the new lines is, it requires its own meeting. Knowing how vital Warehouse and Distribution is to Barkers, as you oversee sending out our products to our customers, I am officially scheduling a meeting to address this issue at seven o'clock tomorrow morning. I would like the entire Warehouse and Distribution Team to attend, as well as all involved managers and supervisors. An email to this effect will be going out later this afternoon, with a list of participants, the time, and the location."

Arthur Afghan stood again, but all he said was, "Thank you, Mr. Boxer," before he sat back down.

Arthur Afghan, Priya Pekingese and Waseem Weimaraner exchanged looks that were at first stunned. They couldn't believe the new boss had moved so quickly to address their concerns. Looking back and forth between his two fellow conspirators, Arthur began to feel smug, and gave Priya and Waseem each a long Afghan smile. Their plan had worked. Finally, someone would listen to them.

Elsewhere in the audience, unnoticed by Arthur Afghan but keenly observed by Bertie Boxer, the managers and supervisors responsible for the Warehouse and Distribution Team looked to each other and scowled. They shifted in their seats, glaring at the dogs on their team. Each dog among them was wondering the same thing: How would they recover from being publicly called out by their staff? In front of the new boss and every other dog at Barkers, no less. The meeting tomorrow morning at seven was going to be miserable for them, they were sure.

Alex Affenphinscher was still standing and he gave a yelp to get Bertie's attention. "We have problems in accounting too," he said. This was met by a murmur of agreement from others on the accounting team. "We want a meeting. Why should only Warehouse and Distribution get a meeting?"

"Us too," said Lorenzo Labrador of Customer Service, jumping to his feet. "We're just as important as Warehouse and Distribution and Accounting. Barkers couldn't stay in business without our top notch Customer Service. We work harder for Barkers than any dog."

This statement set the other dogs to grumbling, and the Customer Service dogs to yapping. Bertie cleared his throat. He didn't want his meeting to lose focus and get out of control. Couldn't every dog see that if they didn't address the issue of savings, soon none of the other issues would matter?

> You can't chew more bones than you have

"Here is what we will do," Bertie said. He didn't raise his voice, but he kept his tone firm, recapturing the attention of every dog. "Designate some dog in your department to gather a list of all of your concerns. This dog will take your list to a meeting with Minnie Westie in K9 Resources, who will document those concerns."

Bertie turned to Minnie Westie, whose Westie ears were perked up in enthusiasm. "Ms. Westie, please schedule these meetings as soon as possible. I will need your review of each department's concerns in two days. I will determine a course of action and respond to your departments by the end of the week. This goes for any and all departments who have concerns. Right now, we need to focus on the point of this meeting; sniffing out savings."

Bertie then went on with his meeting as planned. Impressed by the calm way their new boss handled the slew of complaints, and his quick and decisive plan for addressing them, the employees of Barker's listened to Bertie Boxer with newfound respect. No other dog stood up to interrupt him, and soon everyone was back onboard with their mission of savings.

"What we're here to discuss," Bertie said, "is company savings. I know that every dog here can come up with at least three ideas for savings. Furthermore, I'm sure that your suggestions will be good ones." Bertie knew that a dog would work harder to uphold a good reputation than to build one, so he wanted them all to know that he was already confident in their success.

"And as every suggestion will be a good one, every suggestion will be carefully considered," Bertie continued. "What you suggest will be heard. After this meeting, a Cost Conservation Committee will be established."

Bertie looked around the room, making sure he had the attention of every dog, because the next part of his speech was very important. "Every suggestion for savings, big or small, will be implemented at Barkers. Unless the Cost Conservation Committee can provide me with a very plausible explanation as to why a suggestion would not actually cut costs, I promise, and I do mean *promise*, that each and every idea will become policy."

Bertie could see he had their commitment now. Every dog had good ideas, and every dog liked the thought of having those ideas heard and implemented.

Barkers had developed a culture of not allowing departmental employees to have a voice in policy making and big decisions, as emphasized by what he had heard that very day from the Warehouse and Distribution Team, Customer Service and Accounting.

Bertie wouldn't let things continue as they were. Not only was it unfair to make large-scale changes that would affect every dog without allowing them input, it was the simple truth that a dog who worked a job day in and day out knew more about that specific job than a manager. Every decision should be made in light of the best information they could glean, and sometimes that information must come from the dog who did the job.

He could see every dog was intrigued by his offer, and every dog was thinking. Gary Golden's brows were wrinkled, as they tended to be when he chewed over an idea. Minnie Westie thumped her tail in enthusiasm. Stella Scottie had her Scottie chest puffed out, her eyes bright. Bertie was sure he would get more than three suggestions from her. Even Arthur Afghan and his friends seemed pleased.

You can't play fetch alone

"I have already had a website created," Bertie told them. "This site is available to all Barkers employees, ensuring every dog has equal access to all of the savings ideas and each step of this process. Ideas will be posted on this site as they come in, and there will be weekly updates showing which ideas the committee has approved and which it has, with my permission, dismissed. As head of K9 Resources, Minnie Westie will be Head Musher for this initiative and responsible for managing the website and keeping every dog in the loop."

Bertie gave his best Boxer smile. "I want this process to be completely transparent. Every dog at Barkers will be involved. I expect you all to submit suggestions, and to have the support of every dog for this project. Savings affect the entire company and every dog here. I look forward to being surprised by the number and scope of ideas, and to all of us being surprised by the value of the savings."

Yapping and clapping filled the warehouse as every dog showed their support for Bertie's plan of action, though Bertie knew some dogs were more enthusiastic about the idea than others. Gary Golden, for one, didn't look entirely happy. Minnie Westie, with her usual can-do attitude, was surely the most excited about the idea. Just as surely, Stella Scottie would declare herself the greatest supporter.

Bertie didn't realize how correct his assessment of Gary Golden was, for Gary was feeling decidedly wretched about the idea of more savings. As far as he could tell, he'd already given up many of the things he enjoyed about his job, like free chow and a bottomless expense account. Gary knew that the measures Boss Bertie had already taken at Barkers were helping everyone, including his department, but of course Gary didn't like change. These changes made him nervous and worried, and created an underlying feeling of stress from the belief that nothing would turn out right.

Worried tails don't wag

In no time at all, ideas poured in and the website filled up. Once they put their doggedness to it, most employees came up with even more than three ideas. Minnie organized the ideas carefully, her Westie enthusiasm contagious. Around Barkers, most every dog was pleased with how fast the website filled with ideas and with what a good job Minnie was doing. The head of K9 Resources, most of the dogs thought, was the perfect dog for the job. Only a few harbored secret doubts, but those were more worried about how much the new boss was relying on Minnie and the extra perks she might receive than the real issue at hand; saving Barkers.

Soon enough, the day came for the first of the weekly Cost Savings Meetings. Minnie Westie was in charge of the meeting, but Bertie arrived early, excited to see how the plan was coming along. Minnie was already there, making sure the room was perfect for her important meeting. The members of the Cost Conservation Committee, comprised of middle and upper management representing every department at Barkers, filed into the conference room. Every dog settled in quickly and all ears turned toward Minnie.

Minnie Westie would have been a bit nervous to hold a meeting with so many important dogs, and Boss Bertie, but she was too excited to tell everyone about all of the wonderful savings ideas the dogs had submitted to be worried.

"Let's begin with the first three ideas we had," Minnie woofed, tail wagging enthusiastically. "The ones submitted at the start of this initiative by Bertie Boxer."

Minnie then proceeded to reiterate the suggestions Boss Bertie made during the companywide meeting. She outlined each idea to the committee, from getting rid of unused magazine and newspaper subscriptions, to doing away with ordering snacks for employee only meetings, and on to her favorite, Bertie Boxer's idea about avoiding outside hiring for jobs that dogs at Barkers could already do. There was some grumbling, mostly from Gary Golden, over the snacks but, in the end, all three of Bertie Boxer's ideas were approved.

A good idea can't be buried

"Now," Minnie said, pleased to have such good ideas to present, "we come to a large ticket item. The suggestion has been made that our old headquarters be sold and management moved to a currently unused showroom at Manufacturing Plant A. It's closer to town, and we're paying for both buildings at this time."

"That's out of the question," Berlinda Basset snarled. "Give up our historical headquarters and move to a warehouse? Why, what sort of image would that present? It would be an embarrassment. Who made such a ridiculous suggestion?"

What Berlinda Basset didn't say was that she had worked for years to maneuver into the spacious corner office she now had, and loved bringing people there to show it off. Minnie's tail stopped wagging. Several of the other managers echoed Berlinda Basset's opinion, one even growling under his breath that the dog who had the temerity to offer such a suggestion should be fired.

It's never the mailman's fault

"Hold on now," Boss Bertie said, not liking the direction the barking around the table was headed. That was the sort of dog-brained talk that would stop the ideas from coming in, and Bertie wouldn't have it. "Someone tell me a reason why this idea is good."

For a moment, every dog was silent. Then, Gary Golden said, "It would save on drive time."

Some of the other dogs nodded.

"It's an old building, and zoned as historical," Minnie Westie said. "It costs a lot to maintain it and we can't make some of the energy saving upgrades that would help, because of the zoning."

"That building is the face of Barkers, Inc.," Berlinda Basset snarled. "Why, its façade is on our letterhead."

All around the table, dogs barked back and forth about the building, while Bertie Boxer listened intently. Finally, when they started turning in circles after their own tails, Bertie interrupted once more. "Can any dog tell me a concrete, solid, non-letterhead related reason for why we shouldn't sell the headquarters building?"

Around the table, ears, eyes and noses turned toward Berlinda Basset. She opened her mouth several times, but she couldn't think of a single concrete, solid, practical reason to keep the old building. Finally, she shook her head, her long basset ears flopping from side to side and her big basset eyes drooping with sorrow.

"We promised to implement all good cost saving ideas," Bertie Boxer said. "Unless someone can come up with a good reason not to sell it, the old building must go. Minnie Westie, what is the next idea?"

Minnie hurried on, realizing Boss Bertie wanted to move forward before the arguing could begin anew. She presented several more ideas, pointing out the potential savings of each and giving a timeline for implementation. These ideas, like restricting window cleaning to once a quarter instead of once a month, passed through the committee easily.

As Minnie went over the ideas, which she had broken down by category, Bertie and the other dogs on the Cost Conservation Committee began to realize the huge potential the cost saving initiative had for Barkers. Some of the ideas were small and some were big, but most all of them were good. For some of the managers, it was the first time they dared to let themselves hope they could really turn the company around. Bertie smiled his Boxer smile, pleased with how the initiative was unfolding.

Now that the controversy of the headquarters building had passed, everything continued smoothly, until Minnie brought up the suggestion some dog had made that all Barkers, employees, of any level, fly coach.

Every dog loves his spot in the sun

"No," howled Gary Golden. "First my lunches, then my snacks, and now my first-class flights?" He put his long retriever jaw down on the table and covered his eyes with his paws.

"It would certainly save money," Berlinda Basset said, a little malice in her tone.

"It would indeed," Bertie said, nodding.

"Of course, we all know you wouldn't fly coach, Boss Bertie," Berlinda Basset said. "You're the CEO, after all."

Bertie Boxer shook his head, recognizing a trap when he saw one. He would have to keep an eye on Ms. Basset. "The suggestion was that all dogs at Barkers fly coach," he said. "That includes me."

Around the table, tails thumped happily. It didn't seem so bad to give up something when Boss Bertie was willing to do the same. Only Berlinda Basset looked displeased. She had hoped the new boss would make an exception for himself. She planned to use any special treatment Boss Bertie gave himself, or any other dog, to undermine the plan to sell the headquarters building.

Berlinda Basset was, however, to be disappointed. Bertie Boxer stayed true to his promise. Every idea was considered, and every idea that would save money was implemented. Weeks went by. Ideas poured in and savings piled up.

Bertie Boxer never missed a Cost Conservation Committee meeting and never closed his door to any dog or on any idea. Bertie knew that communication and transparency were the keys to the success of his plan and that he needed to maintain a central role in deciding which ideas to implement if he wanted the plan, and Barkers, to succeed.

A bone in the mouth is worth two buried in the garden

Bertie soon asked Minnie Westie to open every meeting with a quick follow-up on how previously discussed ideas were being implemented and what savings were being achieved. He knew it was one thing to have a good idea, and a different thing entirely to carry it through. Boxer was committed to carrying through his idea of a company-wide, head to tail, approach to savings, and he wanted those implementing each idea to be committed to following through as well. Almost as much as he wanted company savings, Bertie wanted to show how important listening to every dog could be toward not missing opportunities for savings.

Even after the first meeting, it still happened that, on occasion, some dogs on the Cost Conservation Committee tried to resist various changes and suggestions. These instances were sometimes valid, for saving on one thing would cost more somewhere else, but most of the time resistance for a savings idea was based around pet projects or perks.

> *Every dog has a favorite chew toy*

In those cases, Bertie reminded the committee members of the promise he'd made to the dogs of Barkers. He'd stood up before them at the companywide meeting and told them that every cost saving idea would be implemented unless the committee could give him solid, logical reasons why the measure wasn't in the best interest of the company as a whole. Now and then, committee members left the meetings displeased, but Bertie knew that was a small price to pay for saving Barkers.

Overall, most suggestions were approved. Running totals of projected and enacted savings were tabulated on the website and every dog was encouraged to visit it frequently to see the growing savings, as well as to send in any new savings ideas they came up with. It turned out that not only did Bertie Boxer's plan help Barkers' finances, it also improved moral throughout the company. Dogs could see that the new boss was serious when he said he wanted their ideas and promised to listen to them.

As for Arthur Afghan and his friends, they had their morning meeting with Boss Bertie and their supervisors and managers, and they aired their grievances. That morning, they were still so pleased with the success of their plan, and so excited to tell the new boss every detail of what was wrong with their department, that they didn't even notice how their supervisors glared and glowered. Bertie listened carefully to all that was said. He told them he would give every concern proper consideration and develop a course of action.

Bertie, however, had his own goals for the meeting, and they included more than simply hearing the complaints of the Warehouse and Distribution Team. When Arthur Afghan and his friends were finished, Bertie looked around the room at the smug hounds from Warehouse and Distribution, and their irate managers and supervisors. Bertie shook his head.

No biting in the workplace

"I said it was a brave thing for you to stand up before every dog in Barkers and share your concerns," Bertie said to Arthur and his friends, who preened a little. "It was brave, and it did accomplish your goal of progress and change. However, I don't think it is the proper course of action moving forward. Accomplishing change by shaming and undermining others, and interrupting meetings, will never truly benefit the company. As CEO, I strive for every dog at Barkers to feel like one team, working toward one goal; success."

Arthur Afghan and his friends exchanged looks. They hadn't expected this. Glancing around at their managers and supervisors, they finally began to realize the trouble they had caused.

"I never want issues like these to be unaddressed again," Bertie said, to all the dogs present at the meeting. "Moving forward, we all need to communicate better, from the tail of this organization to the nose. Communication and teamwork are our best assets. If there's a breakdown in those, we need to fix it. I expect every dog in this room to give me three suggestions on how we can maintain good communication in this department so that nothing like this happens again."

With that, Bertie thanked everyone and closed the meeting. He returned to his grand old office, which he would soon have to give up as part of the new cost saving program, , and stood before the grand old mirror, adjusting his favorite red tie. Bertie smiled his Boxer smile. So far, they had tackled the culture of superfluous meetings and implemented a plan for savings. Bertie Boxer, the new boss from Britain, was pleased, but he knew there was still a lot to do.

Part Two: The Reality

Savings – Large and Small

Company Savings don't just happen . . .

There are good (positive) ways to make savings and bad (ineffective) processes.

There are many ways to approach cost saving initiatives in a company. I have seen and been part of several different approaches and most, although not all, have been successful.

When asked, employees can always come up with money saving actions in return for a reward or a boost to their professional reputation. Employees not in a position to boost the company's revenue (top line), can, on the other hand, make a difference to the bottom line by suggesting ideas for saving money.

A *positive*, inclusive, approach to making savings gets employees energized and ready to tackle the project.

A *negative*, top down, approach leaves participants wondering why they weren't involved/consulted in the first place and asking themselves why they should participate now.

THE KEY TO ACHIEVING COMPANYWIDE SAVINGS
A plan that involves all management, supervision and employees, with everyone participating toward a common saving goal or initiative.

The least effective schemes I have witnessed have been ones where an 'out of the blue' leadership demand comes down the management chain, with a target for a certain given amount of money to be removed from the budget, without warning or consultation. The result is always the same as employees lose motivation and trust in the department's management team. It's difficult to recover from this type of situation. The challenge then becomes how to explain to the workforce why senior leadership felt they had to act in this way. The workforce is left wondering what superior knowledge and experience senior leadership thought they had that allowed them to know where budgets should be cut, without discussion and input from the operating teams entrusted with the business.

Middle management become the losers in this situation since they are left 'high and dry,' trying to decide whether to go along with the senior management dictate, and appear to support the approach, or sympathize with the operating team. The alternative is to 'stand up' and be critical of the approach, refuse to be associated with the concept dictated by senior level executives, and risk a 'them and us' situation where everybody, and the company, loses because the process is not supported.

This type of hierarchical leadership should be a thing of the past, but it isn't, and there are examples to be seen in many companies even today.

These days, successful companies generally understand that good ideas can come from anywhere in the organization, and not necessarily from the business unit where the savings are to be implemented. They try to make employees feel responsible for their actions and make a point of recognizing their contributions as important, regardless of how big or small the savings may be.

A company that doesn't operate in this manner in today's environment is a tough place to work. If senior management demands that employees throw away their carefully crafted budgets and stop what they're doing to slash expenses without interaction and discussion, it sets up a behavioral style that, in the long run, will not benefit the company. Why would someone want to start a task on his or her own accord, when it is known leadership could come along at any moment and change the scope of work already approved and being implemented?

Savings, in any company, should not rely on just a 'top down' or a 'bottom up' approach but rather a combination of the two, if the maximum opportunity for savings is to be realized.

A company savings plan usually has one of three outcomes:
- The savings are roughly in line with the leadership requirement
    This is likely where a target is set to remove expense to a predetermined level without much consultation with employees.
- The savings fall short of the objective
    This can be the result of an impossible target or a plan not well communicated within the organization
- The savings are greater than anticipated
    This most often results from employees being consulted and engaged upfront, along with good

communication on the task and good communication throughout the process, with the resultant savings visible to all involved.

Examples of savings made by employees that resulted in change in company thinking and procedures:
This first, simple example, is from a marketing employee responsible for a company's exhibitions and trade shows. She recognized the high cost of furniture rentals from their convention supplier. The employee solution included buying furniture from a stylish discount chain for much less than the rental rates. Since the furniture was reusable, it resulted in a savings of tens of thousands of dollars. For this extraordinary effort to save money, the employer gave a reward of $1,000 to the employee.

Another example of employee created savings involves an employee on a business trip to New York who stayed at a friend's place, rather than at a hotel. When the employee was asked why he hadn't submitted a bill for a hotel, it was explained that it was to save money and that everyone in the company should be encouraged to do the same. Following this initiative, the company introduced a 10 percent plan. When employees stayed with friends on a business trip, and avoided hotel expenses, they received 10 percent of the approved hotel rate, paid to them instantly after the trip. This proved to be a significant motivation for employees to save money, to the good of the company.

What is the most common mistake when trying to make savings?
Poor communication. Open communication on the process and decisions made to implement or not

implement company savings ideas is essential to the success of any savings plan.

What is the most common mistake in implementing a savings plan?
Lack of plan leadership. All too often, the plan starts off with a big fanfare and then loses impact because there isn't a central figure managing the process and keeping everyone up to date. A leader of the company, business unit or department needs to play a central role in the savings plan if the savings are to materialize and keep coming. A keen and documented follow up process is essential to make sure that each and every idea is actually put into effect and the savings realized for the company.

How long should a savings program run for?
Some would say that a savings plan or process never ends. In reality, it would need to exist for at least the budget year of the company. This would allow for the savings ideas to be gathered and implementation plans to be put into practice, although all the savings would not be achieved until the second or later years.

A Real Life Example – The Author as CEO

How did the author manage cost savings as a CEO?

I invited all employees at all levels to a meeting on the subject of cost savings. This meeting was scheduled in advance of the company's annual budget setting process. At the meeting I explained that:

- We needed to remove cost from the organization
- We wanted everyone to play a part and contribute to a savings process
- We wanted savings to be proposed no matter how small
- We promised all savings ideas would be implemented if possible
- We committed to keep everyone informed on the progress and success of the savings process
- We promised complete transparency on why any idea would *not* be implemented
- We looked forward to being challenged with new 'out of the box' thinking
- We would set up a Cost Conservation Team (CCT). It would be comprised of all disciplines from the company
- I would be the chair of the CCT
- We would appoint a permanent manager with overall responsibility for the savings process and communication to the organization
- **We challenged all employees to come up with at least three cost saving ideas**

How often did the Cost Conservation Team Meet?

The Cost Conservation Team met formally on two occasions each month, always at the same time and place. The team was comprised of the leaders of all the major functional areas of the company. A central record was kept of all ideas brought forward and the status of the CCT reviews was documented. After each meeting, brief minutes were circulated to all employees.

What was the Agenda of the Cost Conservation Meetings?
Each savings suggestion had to be reviewed by the functional head where the idea impacted most, in advance of the meeting. A recommendation to 'go' or 'not go' with the idea came from the functional head and the annual savings were shown to the CCT. The Cost Conservation Team either challenged the 'not go' or approved the idea to be implemented. Unless there was unanimous agreement not to implement a suggestion, it was returned for further analysis. The manager of the process recorded the annual savings and the decision. At each meeting, we reviewed as many of the suggestions as possible, in the time allotted for the meeting.

How was the communication to all employees handled?
After each of the Cost Conservation Meetings had taken place, the manager of the CCT process sent out an email to all employees with the overall list of suggestions, the decisions of that particular meeting, and the total annual savings approved to date.

Why did this work?
Every employee sees waste in an organization, either in their own department or another. This process enables the organization to accept ideas to save money with new eyes.

What was the largest cost saving idea that was proposed?

We had just refurbished an office building for the company HQ. One of the suggestions was to sell the refurbished office building and remain in the present, less than efficient, office space.

What was a small, but worthy, idea that was proposed?

One of the smaller, yet substantial cost saving, ideas was to cancel all newspaper and magazine publication subscriptions throughout the company. It was found that the majority of the material was available online. It was also discovered that the same publications were being purchased by numerous departments and rarely ever read.

How do you know when all the savings ideas have been tabled?

As each year passes, one constant in any progressive company is the element of change. When you hear from employees that change is very much part of the culture, it is one positive sign that the company is developing and changing to meet the new business environment. Expense that was determined to be essential in a previous business model may be redundant in the new and, unless someone puts a stop to it, the company will continue to spend in the old way without reward. So, there are always going to be ways and means for a company to create savings. The key is to identify them at the earliest opportunity and make the savings timely, avoiding damage to the company's overall performance.

Are there consultant companies that can complete this task for an organization?

There are companies that will help with cost savings and will work for organizations to save both on the supply side and on services, to reduce operating expense. Often, they are associated with buying groups and promise business cost savings from top suppliers. They, for example, negotiate rebate and discount programs with endorsed suppliers for direct and indirect goods and services and reduce operating expenses for its members. However, a consulting company can never offer the breadth and depth of savings that can come from a company's own employees.

Is there a list of cost saving ideas as a reference?
This book includes a list of 100 savings ideas for businesses both large and small. Although every company's needs are different, suggestions on this list may be used directly or as inspiration for ideas that fit your business.

100 Ways to Save Money in Business

1. If you have happy customers, ask them to tell others what they have gained from using your product or services. They can do this in presentations or on social media to encourage others to use your products or services.

2. If you have a complementary neighborhood business, share advertising and promotional costs with them for joint activities. Form a marketing alliance by sharing mailing lists and suppliers that sell complementary products and services.

3. Teach at a class, write an article for local newspapers or speak at local events. This forms the opinion that you are an expert in your field and this attention and opinion will be obtained at low cost with positive results.

4. Use local cable TV stations that have low cost advertising rates at certain time slots during the day and make a personal appearance. Although it is unlikely that this plan will reach prime time viewers it is a cost-effective way to reach consumers in their private homes.

5. Use the point-of-purchase opportunity to the maximum by adding coupons, promotional material and newsletters into the package along with the customer's purchase.

6. Ask your best customers for assistance by giving you referrals and names of specific individuals who have a need for your products and services. Your customers can be a wonderful and reliable source of potential new customers that will increase the percentage and value of business generated by referrals.

7. Organize special events that draw in both new and existing customers and find a related sponsor who will carry the expense of the event. Sponsors will support the event in exchange for some form of advertising within the event and particularly if the two businesses are in the same field.

8. There are many alternatives to traditional advertising and the internet provides different marketing and advertising opportunities which still reach potential customers. Public relations continue to be a cheaper and often a more effective form of advertising for small and large companies alike. Companies can utilize their expertise to get themselves featured as credible sources on TV, radio, in publications and media outlets.

9. The practice of guerilla marketing can be a cost-effective way of finding new customers at low cost. It can also get you noticed, so investigate the opportunities to embark on a guerilla marketing campaign to build your new customer base.

10. Introduce some old-style inexpensive marketing practices to bring in customers who can, in the end, make a huge return. The practice of sending a handwritten thank you note to a customer can increase sales substantially and at a cost of just a stamp and a few minutes of your time.

11. Look for partnerships with other start-up companies to cut costs and increase reach on promotional activities. By partnering with related businesses and making alliances, the benefits far outweigh the alterative of placing an advertisement or a radio spot alone.

12. If you know your customers well it is possible to limit your online marketing efforts and focus your efforts instead on where you know they go online rather than spreading scarce resources over the total area of internet options.

13. By rewarding positive customer behavior with little proactive gestures, it keeps the business environment positive. If it means spending a little money on your best customers who account for the majority of your sales, it is about investing in the relationship that will ultimately bring more profit to the business.

14. It is possible to buy recycled printer cartridges so look into your local newspaper, yellow pages or search Google for a recycled cartridge supplier.

15. When you buy used office equipment you can save more than 60 percent on used office equipment, furniture, computers and copiers. Look into companies that rent or sell office equipment and visit auctions and scan local newspapers for availability of used equipment.

16. Many suppliers of software products offer free trial downloads and limited versions of their full specification products, to get business started with their organization.

17. Instead of buying forms from your local office supply company or creating your own, it is possible to find many free forms online which can be modified to meet your needs and then print.

18. Look for innovative ways to use technology to solve day-to-day inconveniences. Avoid time on administration and sending information back and forth between various parties by utilizing document sharing. It simply speeds up the workflow and increases productivity with no extra business costs.

19. Improve meeting efficiency by asking all participants to explain what they are working on that day. This will improve communications and ensure everyone is on the right track and not wasting time on unnecessary tasks.

20. Hold a short daily meeting with everyone standing up to make sure the group is energized and on point with the needs of the organization.

21. Share office space with other companies to reduce costs by working in an office environment alongside another company for conference rooms, kitchen facilities and co-working spaces.

22. Utilize a corporate credit card program to manage employee expenses which, at the same time provides good quality management information.

23. Use the new generation of portable print and scan technology to support business efficiency improvements and allow productivity when out of the office and to get important documents into the workflow.

24. Develop an office routine to become more efficient with the utilization of time. Use the first two hours of each day to focus on growing the business with your phone and emails turned off. Then allocate the rest of the day in one hour or thirty minute slots and avoid being distracted to stay focused only on that task.

25. Create a folder for each of the days of the week and put into each the tasks that must be completed on that day. Any task that is not completed moves to the next day. This builds a positive routine.

26. Understand the importance of cash flow in business and separate it from profitability. Identify and document your payment process. Keep a list of your key customers and their contact information so that you can check with them within ten days of sending out an invoice if all is in order with the invoice.

27. Always understand your forward order book as a means of controlling cash flow. Only include as confirmed when the order is confirmed and keep separated from probable or possible business.

28. Consider collecting a percentage of cash up front with every purchase. This helps your company improve cash flow, reduce risks and save money in collection activities.

29. Consolidate business insurance to avoid costly time securing individual and multiple quotes for each part of the business. Business owners can make savings by lumping all insurance with one company but need to make sure the comparison is on a 'like for like' basis.

30. Look into consolidating services known as 'bundled services' where companies include a phone service, cable, internet fax and even web hosting. By bundling two or more services from the same company this action can provide measurable savings.

31. Do everything possible to avoid bank fees like ATM charges, bounced check fees and the new debit card fee. If you can cut significant costs by switching to another bank, then this should be considered.

32. Utilize a debit card payroll system to reduce administrative costs by eliminating the expense associated with printing checks and at the same time avoid or limit the opportunity for fraud.

33. To avoid high investment costs at 'start up' when purchasing equipment, consider a lease since this will conserve your company's cash flow and save a considerable amount of money in repairs and maintenance.

34. Offer your customers electronic invoicing by email (e-invoicing) direct to your customers. This will reduce your company's print and postage costs.

35. Set guidelines for employee spending and activate pre-set credit card spending limits and alerts. Also, monitor monthly spending reports to save money and avoid out of line expense.

36. Ask your suppliers if they provide discounts and what the requirements are for a lower pricing. Determine if you are able to meet the suppliers' requirements in order to qualify for a better price or other incentives like an interest free loan or a vendor credit. Some suppliers have a plan which provides a discount for paying early.

37. It is possible to transfer a debt balance from one credit card to a 0% introduction APR card as a way to save money on interest charges and pay down a debt. The savings in interest charges can be substantial and will help with cash flow over the period.

38. By moving to a paperless company, it is possible to reduce storage and printing costs and simultaneously improve the overall efficiency of the company. By scanning and sharing information electronically it will save time and money as well as efficiency.

39. Many vendors are often willing to negotiate lower prices rather than lose a regular customer. What a business has been paying to a vendor over a period does not have to be the final price forever, so before looking for a new supplier, negotiate with the existing one to lower the cost.

40. Keep full-time staff to a minimum and outsource to independent contractors the work your full-time staff cannot cover as required. Employee costs from salaries to office space and benefits are expensive and are often the largest expense for a small business.

41. The implementation of telecommuting is not possible for all companies and not for all employees. When it is suitable for both the company and its employees it can become a large area for saving in terms of expense. By keeping things virtual, it will allow a small business to avoid expense for office space and its supporting operating costs. A plan to do work with the minimum operating cost is the focus for telecommuting and even if it is not feasible for all employees, implement for those areas where it will work to cash in on the savings.

42. Negotiate with the landlord of your building for a lower lease to save on costs. This is one of the largest expenses for a small business, so negotiating a better deal will bring big savings to the bottom line.

43. If you go green in the office it can also be a smart move financially. For example, replacing the existing printer with one that prints on both sides of the paper to save paper, or keeping office equipment on a power strip to be turned off when not in use to save power, all contribute to a green policy which is not just great PR.

44. Review the office cleaning services and determine if it is necessary to be done daily or would a weekly service be acceptable. At the same time, review the frequency of maintenance costs to save money without reducing necessary service areas completely.

45. Make a point of reviewing and comparing prices on shipping and negotiate the best possible rates to save every possible amount. A small saving on each package shipped will add up to a considerable savings amount over a year.

46. Review the number of meetings held in the organization and look for duplication of tasks. On-site meetings can be expensive both in terms of travel and hosting costs and even virtual meetings come at a cost of billable hours or salary expense. Limit the number of people who are required to be at the meetings and make sure the employees time is well spent by being there.

47. Look into all expenses both large and small. Review all expenses to cut out anything unnecessary. Small cuts in ongoing expenses can add up to substantial saving over the longer term.

48. It is always possible to find a cheaper way to provide the same employee benefits. Be a lean profit generating company by reviewing everything from office water cooler expense to how many glossy office magazines are ordered in duplicate for the offices.

49. Review your company's distribution process to find ways to simplify or eliminate the processes. Keep the focus of the employees on growing the business and negotiate agreements which keep the business moving forward. It may not be the best practice for your company to do the distribution itself and an alternative such as a 'drop shipment' arrangement with your supplier could be a more cost-effective method.

50. Consider hiring temporary employees to handle the business at a time of short- term surges in the business such as Christmas in the retail trade. This avoids employees who can sit idle when business is slow.

51. Avoid full-time staff and consider running your office as a home-based entrepreneur. You can use an executive suite which meets a variety of needs including access to a private mailbox, and a receptionist to answer or forward calls to your home office.

52. Hold off on signing a 3-10 year lease for a permanent retail location and use a kiosk, cart or a temporary space to test your product and marketing concepts. The upfront cost of a kiosk or cart is far less than fitting out a retail shop and has much less associated risk. If the concept or location doesn't work you are still mobile and can try a new location or switch marketing plans.

53. Keep down costs when setting up an online retail store and use low cost online auction sites such as eBay and Yahoo. It is possible to create a professional storefront look by using 'website in a box' solutions which can be organized for a reasonable monthly fee.

54. Find customers for your product or services inexpensively by researching your market to find potential visitors for your website. View the Usenet news groups which are forums for the internet, where people post messages for public viewing. Also, special interest groups related to your market, product or service can be found.

55. Use your free time to start chatting online by finding newsgroups that cater to your audience for products and services, and jump into the discussion to generate business. All it costs is your time and energy. Always include your URL in your signature and provide helpful information to make people want to click on your website.

56.   Your URL is an important calling card so always use it on your letterhead and business cards and in all email signatures. Don't forget to also put it on all promotional material, uniforms, press releases and company vehicles. In fact, anywhere potential visitors will see it.

57.   Use the US Postal Service to help you clean up your mailing list. It is a free service and they help with correcting addresses, pointing out incomplete addresses and adding Zip plus 4 numbers, to take advantage of bar code discounts.

58.   Organize an alternative place to run your business just in case of some unforeseen disaster. Have this back up plan to save on Business interruption insurance. Perhaps a company in the same industry would be a place to locate your business on a temporary basis.

59.   It is possible to save when buying insurance upfront since it saves money in the long run. One area where businesses should not cut corners is in the area of Disaster Recovery. Talk to your insurance company about which situations would have a potential catastrophic impact on your business and take out adequate insurance.

60.   If you raise the deductible amount on your insurance, it usually means a lower premium. If you make a claim you will end up paying the higher deductible but it is likely to be far less than the amount that you save.

61. When you enter into employee leasing, this means you are handing over your workforce to a professional organization with experience in this field. This organization then leases your employees back to you and you save substantially on employee benefits.

62. Many retired employees are willing to contribute their experience, knowledge and time at low cost. This can be a huge benefit to growing and organizing a small business.

63. Local college students are a potential resource for help and can be employed as interns for minimal costs, at the same time learning the business.

64. If you deliver your mail to the post office early in the morning, experience shows you can get one to two-day delivery for the price of a first-class stamp.

65. If the time of delivery of your product is not crucial within a day or two, avoid expensive overnight charges and opt for an extra day service to save money.

66. You can avoid the cost of company cars by using the services of companies like Zipcar so that you only pay for the actual time when the car is in use.

67. Business owners can take advantage of Skype which provides free telephone calls between people who have downloaded its software and can save money on long or

International calls. It can also be used for instant messages.

68. If you need a process for important conference calls you may also use the services of freeconferencecalls.com

69. An inexpensive way to engage with your customers is to create a social media platform with Twitter and Facebook as a way to spread the word about your business. Grow your business by listening and learning.

70. Use LinkedIn to inexpensively build your business network, find customers and possibly find new staff.

71. When your business is conducted in coffee shops and restaurants make sure you utilize these deductions. When you entertain clients or potential customers to discuss business on a service or project, you can deduct a part of your entertainment bill. You must keep an updated log of all entertainment related expenses. You can also deduct a fixed cost per mile for mileage driven when conducting company business. The amount to be charged changes each year so your accountant will advise you on this.

72. If you manage your business credit cards with an unpaid balance at the end of each monthly period, look around for a card with a low interest rate. If it is your procedure to always pay your credit card balance in full it should be important to find a card without an annual fee or at least one with a longer grace period. If you ask a credit card issuer to waive the annual fee or reduce the interest rate some will cooperate and particularly if you tell them other companies are attempting to get your business with more favorable rates and without annual fees.

73. Try to avoid asking credit card companies for a cash advance as they normally charge an upfront fee of more than 2 percent of the advance and also start accruing interest immediately.

74. When you make deposits to your bank try to make it early in the morning so that you get credit and start to earn interest immediately.

75. Don't wait for your suppliers to deliver your order if their location is close to your business. Ask friends or family members to collect it and save on shipping costs. Only pick it up yourself if it doesn't take you away from sales-generating business.

76. If you can, make every effort to avoid giving your customers credit. If you feel you have to offer credit, then check out the customer's credit worthiness in detail in advance.

77. Try swapping one of your products or services with those of another company is a good way to conserve cash or get rid of unwanted slow moving inventory.

78. Whatever you buy, be it large or small, do it only after you have received three quotes from three different suppliers. By shopping around, you will find out the real market price, and if you have a preferred supplier they are likely to want to match your lowest quote to earn your business.

79. Try to avoid paying consultants to do the things you can do yourself, or internally in your company. It is possible to hire a consultant for an hour or so to teach you how to do such things as press releases or promotions, so that in the future you can handle it in house.

80. Don't ignore any written or phone complaints. Try to work out any problems before they grow into bigger ones and avoid lawsuits.

81. If you have to hire an attorney, make sure you have an agreement on what is and what is not included in the arrangement to avoid any surprises later. Your agreement should include an estimate of the time to be spent on your particular case as well as what is covered, including typing and photo copying, and specifically, what is not included.

82. When and if you have consultants working for you in the organization, there comes a time when you will need to barter with them on the costs of their services. It is sometimes helpful to ask the very consultants you have employed to come up with ideas on how you can cut back on their costs. Ask your insurance agent and accountant the very same question. In the end, you will be surprised by the positive response you will receive.

83. It is possible to order checks from a printing company and they can sometimes be cheaper than ordering them through a bank.

84. Some suppliers are keen to give a discount for early payment. Others don't provide any incentive to settle early, and in these instances, it is to your advantage to pay your bills for suppliers, utilities and taxes as late as possible, as long as you do not incur a fee. Having the money under your own control means it is earning for you until the last minute.

85. Always track your 'petty cash' as though you don't need to have receipts for items with a value of less than $100.00; over a 12-month period this can add up. So, it makes sense to still track these expenses.

86. If you manage your business from a home office it is possible to deduct a part of your rent or mortgage interest and utilities as a business expense. It is also possible to deduct a percentage of the cost of services which includes house cleaning, lawn care and home maintenance.

87. An opportunity to save cost often rests in the area of outside storage, where for convenience an off-site storage unit is rented on a monthly basis to house records or perhaps slow moving/obsolete inventory. Try to get rid of this space by selling of the stock and finding other methods of data storage to avoid this expense.

88. By joining an industry association, as a member you are entitled to have access to special terms and discounts on travel, insurance and car rental in return for a small membership fee.

89. If you have established a business with a friend or family member as a partnership it is important to have a partnership agreement in place right from the start. This will avoid costly disruptive issues in the future.

90. Talk to other business owners and share money saving tips with people who have succeeded in the world of business. You will get ideas on how to lower your overheads, meet target costs and build a profitable business. The plan is to always lower your monthly operating costs and trying new ideas can bring positive rewards.

91. When it comes to making charitable contributions, it is possible to remove them all together and record the savings. It may also make sense to review charitable contributions and come up with an agreed policy on just what, when and where contributions will be approved. By the policy being available to all employees it is easier to communicate consistently on all requests for donations.

92. Some businesses can benefit from the introduction of a shorter four-day working week when the organization saves on utility and operating costs. Not all employees need to be reduced to the shorter week, which saves on salary costs for the business in total.

93. Interns hired from local schools can help build a business' social media platform. By using their expertise on Facebook and Twitter on a regular basis they can help to bring in more business. They can also utilize and optimize search engine formulas at a fraction of the cost of full-time employees.

94. If it has been your habit to send birthday cards or other special event cards through the mail to each of your retail customers, consider if sending an email would be more targeted, timely and still be just as effective. Postage and card costs can be expensive and emailing would be a considerable savings.

95. Office supplies can be expensive so it makes sense to switch to shopping for less expensive deals on items such as ink printer cartridges sourced from bulk warehouses or online suppliers. Review how you randomly purchase these items and end up paying the high price of having local convenience when you go to middle man suppliers.

96. Don't book a conference room for a meeting when on the road unless you have to. Use quiet hotels, business spaces, customers' offices, or coffee shops to do business on the move.

97. Register domain names cheaply online. The price at www.godaddy.com starts from just a few dollars.

98. If you are planning to hold a celebration event for sales achievement or some other goal-related success, combine it with a training day to make full use of the facility and having all your employees available.

99. Most business owners have underperformers in the organization and every department seems to have one of them. Management knows their work hasn't been satisfactory but feels uncomfortable about dismissing them. So, take the personnel action you have most likely been avoiding for some time, which is reassigning or terminating the underperformers.

100. Work on the basis that every aspect of business is negotiable and set out to make improvements in every functional area, to the benefit of your business and that of your customers.

Book Three

BARKERS ON GROWTH

INTRODUCTION

Many a manager has been asked by his boss, "How can we develop and implement business growth opportunities in the organization?" This is not an easy question to answer.

Increasing revenue is not the easiest of tasks and attempting it requires the organization to form a new plan. To do this, a number of very important decisions must be made about how the company will operate in the future. There are questions concerning the allocation of resources and budgets, and who will be tapped or called in to introduce the growth strategy. Also, how will the existing business respond to the potential disruption of a new plan?

No growth strategy will work unless it is embraced by the organization. Without support, a new plan will not get off first base.

I always found that when you ask your organization to dream and imagine the future of the business, you get some surprising results. It helps to establish the direction of the organization and helps with the "How do we get there?" question.

In my opinion, the easiest way to seek out potential opportunities to grow a company's revenue stream is to look into the existing resources within the organization. Bertie Boxer also has his own way of seeking out business opportunities, as you will read in the following story.

PART ONE: THE STORY

Boss Bertie Boxer, the new CEO of Barkers, Inc., was at his dapper best for the All-Day Manager and Supervisor Meeting. He had on his favorite bow tie, which he'd tied himself, and was well and freshly groomed. He was also bright eyed, but not bushy tailed, as he was a Boxer, after all.

Always aware of how the setup of a room could affect a meeting, Bertie arrived early to survey the room. Seeing the tables and chair set out in a long row, he quickly rearranged the furniture into an open square to ensure every dog would have a good view of every other. He also removed any unwanted distractions and cleared the large corkboard covering one wall of the room. Once he was satisfied with the setting, Bertie distributed felt pens and pads of notepaper. He then scrubbed both sides of the whiteboard clean. On one side, he wrote, in large clear letters, *What's going well here?*

Boss Bertie then stood back and waited for the managers and supervisors of Barkers to arrive. Before long, dogs began to amble in. Bertie observed carefully which dogs arrived early and which late. He noted which preferred to sit near the front of the room, displaying their dominance, enthusiasm or ego, and which sat near the back, a sign of subservience or a dog who didn't want to attract attention or participate. Lastly, Bertie took special note of which dogs brought kibbles into the meeting, something he'd expressly forbidden. Chow was too great of a distraction for any dog.

A dog with a bone always drools

Stella Scottie, Bertie's one-time critic, marched right to the front of the room, sitting near the boss. Minnie Westie, a bright spot of enthusiasm at Barkers, headed for the front as well, though she didn't seem to mind that Stella was already there, her Scottie ears standing tall as she glanced about with bright eyes. Gary Golden, Head of Sales, sat almost as far from Bertie as he could. Gary, a known chowhound, didn't bring in any food of his own, but looked longingly at the few biscuits and bones on the table.

As more dogs filed in, Bertie checked his watch. Promptly on time, he began the meeting, sending those dogs lingering on the fringes seeking their seats. "This morning, I would like to get a feel for what's going well at Barkers. You'll notice in front of you ample notepaper and pens. I want every dog here to write out anything they can dig up about what's going well at Barkers."

Some dogs, like Minnie Westie, and Stella Scottie, reached for pens and notepaper immediately, writing with enthusiasm. Others, like Gary Golden, let out huffing sighs and set to work. Others still looked around at each other, clearly feeling disdain for the idea. However, under the watchful bright-Boxer eyes of the new CEO they, too, soon began to write. Bertie noticed this last group was made up mostly of those who had disobeyed the new rules and brought in chow.

"Each time you finish an idea, pass it to me," Bertie said. "It's time to see what's going right."

As he got the first pieces of notepaper, Bertie took them to the corkboard, reading them aloud as he pinned each one up for all to see. Spurred on, some by tail-wagging enthusiasm and some by the need to be top dogs, every dog began to write more. Bertie nodded his head, pleased.

Soon, the wall was filling up with statements about what was going well at Barkers. Every manager and supervisor did their best to highlight the merits and achievements of their area of responsibility. Some chests began to get quite puffed out with doggie pride, while others struggled. Bertie kept reading the notes aloud, urging every dog to think hard. No success or achievement was too small.

Bertie, as keen-eared as any guard dog, was aware of a certain amount of grumbling. Although he was reading, and pinning, he could still pick out several dogs moaning and yapping. The warble of one in particular, Billy Beagle, was the loudest.

Bertie recognized Billy Beagle as a dog who came in late, brought food, and sat at the middle of the table. Undiscouraged, for Boss Bertie had dog years of experience implementing the sort of meeting he'd planned for the day, he kept right on reading and pinning. Meanwhile, Billy Beagle chomped on the chow he'd brought and kept right on yapping and whining.

Grumpy dogs chew on the furniture

When the pens stilled and the final note was pinned up, Bertie faced the dogs at the table. "Good work," Bertie said, smiling at the other dogs with his Boxer smile. "Now, I need two volunteers."

Minnie Westie's paw went up, as did Head of Product Development Charles Chihuahua's. Gary Golden sank lower where he sat, doing his best to disappear.

"Minnie, Charles, thank you. Come up to the board," Bertie said. "It's time to organize what's going well here at Barkers. The two of you will read the notes. We'll all agree on how to sort them. Similar notes go together."

Minnie Westie and Charles Chihuahua nodded, trotting up to stand beside Bertie.

Some notes, Bertie knew, were unintelligible due to poor or confusing writing. These he hadn't read aloud earlier, but had pinned up with the rest. In view of them, he added, "If you come to a note you can't read, hold it up." Bertie looked out at every dog in the meeting room. "If your note is held up, please clarify what achievement you want every dog to know about."

This made some dogs worry. Though some dogs had written poorly because writing wasn't their best trick, other had done so on purpose, to hide their lack of enthusiasm for the project or lack of real success to be proud of. A few dogs squirmed.

136

Each note was read aloud again, this time by Bertie's volunteers, and suggestions were voiced as to what notes went together. Even with the interruptions to have some notes explained, every dog soon became involved in deciding how to sort them. Yapping filled the room as dogs tried to get the attention of Bertie's volunteers. More than once, Bertie called on the dogs present to remember that part of being a good meeting participant was listening and giving each dog a chance to be heard. Even with all the yapping, the notes got sorted and a pattern soon emerged as they were moved across the board. Finally, all of the notes were read, with the end result being seven distinct groups.

"Well done," Bertie told the dogs at the meeting. "Now, it is time to think about what you wrote, and what you heard. We need to categorize these notes, and every dog should be in agreement as to what categories there are. What are the major areas of business within Barkers, represented here on the corkboard?"

The dogs looked about at each other, no dog wanting to be first.

> No one
> trusts a
> timid hound
> to guard
> their house

Finally, Minnie Westie raised her paw.
"Minnie?" Bertie asked.
"K9 Resources," Minnie replied.
"Manufacturing," Stella Scottie snapped, her paw shooting up.

Other dogs started barking out answers. Bertie had to call the meeting to order once more, reminding them that every dog should have a chance to speak, but it wasn't long before seven categories of business at Barkers were agreed upon to represent the seven groups of notes. They were: Communications, K9 Resources, Sales and Marketing, Manufacturing, Engineering, Teamwork, and Logistics. Bertie wrote these on their own pieces of notepaper, pinning one above each group of notes on the board.

"Excellent work," Bertie said, once more smiling at the other dogs with his Boxer smile. "You've all done well thinking of successes, sorting them, and coming up with categories. Every dog pulled together like a team. We now have a good idea of what's going well at Barkers."

Many dogs looked about at each other, pleased. Stella Scottie wagged her short Scottie tail. Most dogs weren't sure why they had worked all morning on what was going well but they felt a sense of accomplishment regardless.

"Now, I think it is time for every dog to have lunch," Bertie Boxer said. "We'll meet back here in one hour. Make sure you use your chow time for kibbles, because there is to be no food in this meeting room when we return." Bertie leveled his Boxer stare on more than one dog as he spoke, reminding them who had brought food into the meeting that morning. When the managers and supervisors filed out to get their kibble, some tails weren't wagging.

Bertie Boxer, who skipped the Barkers chow hall for lunch, wouldn't have been surprised by the talk going on there. Some dogs, like Minnie Westie, had tail-wagging enthusiasm for the meeting that morning. Some, like Stella Scottie, didn't know what the meeting was for, but would assume guard dog duty for anything

138

Bertie Boxer did. Others, like Billy Beagle, were happy to be out from under the watchful eyes of the new CEO so they could yap about what they really thought of his meeting.

Wagging tongues often lead to sagging tails

"What a waste of our time," Billy Beagle warbled in his yodeling beagle way, setting down his tray at a table filled with friends. "Why are we looking at what's going well? We should be making lists of what needs fixing. We could have spent the morning problem solving."

Some of the other dogs at the table barked their agreement. Others focused on their chow. They had heard Billy warble before and knew Boss Bertie came to Barkers with years of experience behind him.

"The whole thing is a joke," Billy Beagle continued, in between bites of kibble. "Most of those notes about what's going well are nothing. Every dog is just trying to look good in front of the new boss. They're all prancing about like they're in a show ring. Half those departments are really underperforming."

Lorenzo Labrador of Customer Service, who was on Billy's weekend Frisbee team, looked up from the bone he was gnawing. "Why can't the new CEO see that's what they're doing? It seems as clear as cats' eyes to me."

"I think it's good to look at success," Head of Engineering Lucia Lowchen said. "I feel better about Barkers' future already."

"How can you feel better?" Lorenzo asked. "We haven't spent any time on the issues facing us. We haven't resolved anything."

"After lunch, I'm going to give this new boss a piece of my mind," Billy Beagle warbled.

Around him, some of the other dogs yapped their approval. Others did not, but Billy only heard the yapping ones.

Don't bite the hand that leads you

Bertie Boxer had a quick lunch, having dished up his kibble in advance. He was soon back in the meeting room, readying for the second half of the meeting. He took down the notes, preserving the groupings so that a record could be made later. He made sure pens were still distributed evenly and put out fresh pads of notepaper.

Satisfied with the state of the meeting room once more, Bertie Boxer went to the front of the room and erased his whiteboard. On the clean board, in bold clear letters, he wrote, *What can we do to improve our business and grow in the future?* He turned the board over, so the blank side was showing, knowing the words would be a distraction during the opening of the meeting.

Bertie sat back and waited for the department heads and supervisors to return. This time, fewer were late. They all sat where they had earlier. Only Billy

Beagle and his friend Lorenzo Labrador brought in chow.

Bertie waited for everyone to be seated then addressed the room, saying, "Thank you all for your time and hard work this morning. Before we move on, does any dog have questions about the first half of the meeting?"

"Where did the Post It notes go?" Lucia Lowchen asked, looking around the room, her nose sniffing.

Several other dogs barked interest in the location of the Post it notes as well.

"They have been taken down to be transcribed and circulated," Bertie said, pleased by how many dogs wagged their tails at the news. "Minnie Westie, I am counting on you to see to that."

Her stubby Westie tail thumping, Minnie agreed she would handle that.

"Are there any other questions?" Boss Bertie asked.

Billy Beagle raised his paw to get Bertie Boxer's attention.

"Yes, Billy?" Boss Bertie asked. Being an intelligent Boxer, with experience under his collar, Boss Bertie suspected Billy would try to cause trouble, but he didn't mind. Bertie Boxer from Britain knew that tongues wagged at least as much as tails. It was best to get every dog's worries out of the doghouse and into the yard, for all to see.

"This is all a waste of time," Billy barked. "Barkers has real problems. We should be talking about those. All this talk about what's going right, it's not helping. It's not even true. Look at Minnie Westie's notes, all about how wonderful K9 Resources is. She's talking nonsense, exaggerating her department's achievements to look good in front of every dog, especially you. Why did we waste a morning letting dogs brag when we have real issues to discuss?"

Minnie Westie listened, her tail stilling and her Westie ears dropping. Stella Scottie, beside her, bared her formidable Scottie teeth. It was clear she was ready to snap at Billy for belittling Minnie and doubting Boss Bertie.

There are no
bad dogs,
only bad
behaviors

Unperturbed, Bertie Boxer regarded Billy Beagle with his usual Boxer calm. "Thank you, Billy, for being so honest with your thoughts. I'm sure you're voicing the opinion of others here as well. It's brave of you to speak up. Never fear, I think the afternoon I have planned will please you, addressing your concerns."

Billy preened, his tail wagging. He hadn't expected Boss Bertie would appreciate how brave he was for speaking up. He'd expected the new CEO from Britain to be angry. Billy puffed out his beagle chest, letting out a happy warble. Beside him, Lorenzo Labrador looked envious of the attention Billy was receiving.

"However," Bertie Boxer continued in those same unflappable tones, "in the future, whenever possible, I ask you to refrain from turning your concerns for a process into personal attacks. There was no reason to make specific mention of the notes from K9 Resources. Every dog here was encouraged to dig up any achievement, no matter how small."

Billy Beagle sank back on his haunches, trying to make himself as small as some of the successes Minnie Westie and the others had written down. Every dog was looking his way, and now none of them wore envy on their doggie faces. All around the conference room, dogs panted in distress, their tails still. No dog wanted to see the new CEO angry, or watch another dog get put in a kennel. Even Stella Scottie felt a bit bad for Billy now.

Boss Bertie, a clever a Boxer, would never bite a dog while he was down. Instead, he looked around the conference room, making sure he had the attention of every dog, which he did. It was time to let the managers and supervisors of Barkers know what type of agility course their new boss wanted them to run. "The success or failure of Barkers will be a team effort. We will pull this company out of the doghouse together, or all sleep out in the cold. I expect a one-team, one-sled approach from you all and won't accept any inter-pack rivalry."

Bertie Boxer could see the sad dog eyes all around him, but he knew he'd said what needed to be said. He went to his whiteboard, offering his Boxer smile to reassure the other dogs. Bertie knew the sooner they moved on with the meeting, the sooner every dog would forget the need for Billy's reprimand. Once the work got going, they would be a happy pack.

The lead dog is alone at the head of the pack

143

Bertie turned over the whiteboard, revealing the words he'd written after eating lunch, *What can we do to improve our business and grow in the future?* "Earlier, we unearthed everything that's going well for Barkers. Now, it's time to bark about what we can do to improve our business and grow in the future. You'll notice you have fresh notepads and pens."

Tails started wagging almost immediately. Every dog liked to be a good dog, but every dog also liked to bark about things. Bertie could see their enthusiasm and suspected the managers and supervisors of Barkers had many ideas on ways the company could improve.

"I want every dog to write down anything they can dig up about what we can do better," Bertie continued. "Ideas from every dogs' department are needed, but also for the company as a whole. Every suggestion needs to be brought to heel. This is your opportunity to bark about any ideas you've kept leashed, dreaming of the day you get to parade them before the top dogs at Barkers."

There was an immediate flurry of activity as Post it notes were filled in. The room was silent except for the sound of felt-tipped pens scratching on notepaper and tails thumping. Bertie was unsurprised when notes began coming to the front faster than during the first half of the meeting. Every dog liked to bark at something, be it a strange noise in the building or the approach of the mailman.

Bertie again pinned the notes to the board. He read some aloud any time he heard the sound of pens slackening. Each time, the suggestions he read spurred a new flurry of writing as other dogs were inspired by what they heard. "Don't be shy," Bertie Boxer told the dogs at the meeting. "The only bad idea is an unshared one. Even a watchdog can't hear an idea that's only between your ears."

Soon, the corkboard was nearly covered, with more notes trickling in. Finally, when no more space was left on the board, every dog stopped writing. Bertie smiled his Boxer smile, pleased with the number of suggestions on the board. He again asked for volunteers. Minnie Westie and Lorenzo Labrador were first to raise their paws.

"Minnie, Lorenzo, thank you," Bertie said. "Please come up to the board. Read the notes, asking for clarification if needed, and we'll all pull together to sort them into like groups."

Minnie read a suggestion aloud, the dogs barking about what it meant. Lorenzo read another, moving it to a different section of the board. Minnie took a third, Lorenzo a fourth, and so on for a fifth and sixth note.

Minnie took a seventh, tilting her fuzzy Westie head to the side in question. "This is very much the same flavor as one of the others. Should I read it?" she yapped.

"Yes," Bertie Boxer said. "Read it, and if we all agree it is the same flavor, we'll pin them together. Thick piles of notepaper will show us the areas with the greatest potential for improvement."

Minnie read the note. Every dog agreed it was similar to an earlier suggestion. She pinned it on top of that note and they continued on. There was excitement in the room as every dog worked on sorting the suggestions. The sorting went quicker than that morning as every dog already knew the process and they all worked together to get the task done. Every now and again, Bertie Boxer had to stop side discussions on the merits of any one suggestion and keep dogs on the task of grouping the notes, but overall the managers and supervisors worked like a champion team.

> *Pull the sled in one direction and you'll get there faster*

When the notes were sorted, every dog was surprised at how quickly the task was done, and how it seemed more like a walk in the park than a working dog's day. Pleased with how well the meeting was going, Bertie adjusted his favorite bowtie. "Now is the time to choose a heading for each group," he barked.

This, too, was accomplished with the speed of a greyhound. In fact, the headings used that morning worked as well for how to improve as they had for where things were going well. The notable addition was an eighth heading, Management. This was a dog catcher's net for suggestions which crossed functional lines and required Boss Bertie himself to investigate the feasibility of their implementation.

"Now we need more volunteers," Bertie barked. "Who are the best kibble counters here?"

Alex Affenphinscher of Accounting put up his paw. Then, to every dogs' surprise, so did Gary Golden. Gary had been enjoying sorting notes with his fellow dogs so much, getting to know dogs he rarely or never saw, that he forgot his mantra that any attention from the boss was bad attention. In fact, as the dogs who had brought chow into the meeting room has long since eaten it, and sorting notes had been so engaging, for once, Gary had even forgotten about sniffing out snacks.

"Right then," Bertie Boxer said. "Each of you take a pile and count how many Post Its there are. I need more volunteers for the other piles."

Soon, Bertie had set a whole pack of dogs counting. They counted the afternoon piles, and the morning piles, being careful not to mix them up. While they counted, Bertie cleared the whiteboard again, making two rows with eight headings. One row said, *What are we doing well here?* The other said, *What can we do to improve our business and grow in the future?* As the dogs counted up the notes, Bertie filled in their tallies on the board. When all of the numbers were up, every dog could see there were nearly twice as many ideas for improving Barkers as there were suggestions on what was going well.

Bertie turned from the board, wearing his boxer smile. "With so many suggestions for how to improve, I am confident we can move forward, bringing positive change and growth to the company."

Buried bones keep till a rainy day

Tails wagged and tongues lolled out of doggie smiles. From a giant wolfhound to a miniature poodle, every dog was pleased. Every dog knew growth would bring more treats for all, and every dog liked treats. Gary Golden looked fondly at the number in the category he'd counted, pleased he'd helped put up such good news.

"Now, we have one more task," Boss Bertie said.

All around the room, doggie ears perked up, curious what more Boss Bertie would ask.

"We must have a pack leader for each of our eight areas where we can work harder to be top dogs of the K9 accessories industry," Bertie said. "We also need a pack with the experience and understanding to see each idea carried through. I volunteer to head one team, Management. There are seven more areas for us to agree upon."

Boss Bertie, of course, knew that not every idea in every category would be implemented. Some would prove too costly. Others would, under scrutiny, be labeled as not the best bones in the batch. Bertie knew now wasn't the time to bark about that, though. Now was a time to bark about how well every dog was doing and keep the momentum of the meeting moving forward. Happy dogs were hardworking dogs, and hardworking dogs won more bones.

For the remainder of the meeting, every dog focused on who would be top dog for each group, and what dogs would be on their teams. Most choices for leaders were clear, like Minnie Westie heading the K9 Resources Team, Gary Golden championing the Sales and Marketing Team and Stella Scottie being in charge of the Manufacturing Team. In fact, it was Billy Beagle who suggested Minnie Westie as a team leader, his beagle jowls wobbling as he offered her name by way of an apology for his earlier snapping and snarling. For all his Beagle yowling, Billy, like every dog at Barkers, knew Minnie Westie was a blue-ribbon manager.

Even with many easily sighted choices, each area's champion was carefully discussed, and the members who should be on their team. Bertie was pleased to see this portion of the meeting wasn't permitted to zip by like a sight hound after a rabbit. For a team to succeed, it was important to have the right balance of experience, skills and authority.

Once the teams were agreed upon, Bertie watching carefully to note the strengths and skills of every dog there, Bertie again addressed the Managers and Supervisors of Barkers. "Every dog here has done excellent work today," Bertie said. "Now that we know what we can do better, and have teams for each area where we can improve, each team will research, plan and implement the improvements suggested for their group. Each team will also submit weekly updates on their progress."

The dogs at Barkers looked around, nodding their doggie heads, those with pricked ears and floppy ears alike. Dogs with rough coats and smooth, long tails and short, all watched Boss Bertie with interest.

"From now on," Bertie Boxer continued, "I will chair a monthly meeting to review how each pack is implementing the ideas in their area. After the meetings, updates will be delivered so every dog who worked on what we can do better today can see how well we all pull together."

Bertie Boxer gazed out over the dogs, all types and breeds, who made up the meeting. Some were toy sizes and some giant. There were sight hounds and scent hounds, terriers and hunters and herders. Bertie knew that every dog had strengths and skills to offer Barkers.

"Thank you all for your hard work today," Bertie said. "Every dog here contributed ideas during the meeting. We've shown how well we can come together as one pack and, in doing so, have created a plan of action that will bring real growth. I look forward to helping make that happen."

Dogs barked and yapped, pleased with the success of the meeting. Even Billy Beagle realized he'd been too quick to judge the new boss from Britain. The Managers and Supervisors left their meeting knowing that if they worked as a team, the whole of Barkers could pull ahead together.

Part Two: The Reality

Growth – What's Going Well in the Organization?

What can we do to improve our business and *Grow* in the future?

BUSINESS GROWTH: A DEFINITION FROM THE BD BUSINESS DIRECTORY
The process of improving some measure of an enterprise's success, business growth can be achieved either by boosting the top line of revenue of the business with greater product sales or service income, or by increasing the bottom line or profitability of the operation by minimizing costs.

What's going well in the organization?
My experience in business has shown me the value of remembering to ask the most basic question. These questions aren't complex, and often don't require complicated answers. A good question doesn't have to be veiled in secrecy so as to catch out the receiver. Good questions will often lead to other questions and help those involved achieve true understanding.

In the story you have just read, the first question asked by Bertie is, "What's going well in the organization?" Recently, I read the article *What's Going Well?* by Natalie Houston in the *Chronicle of Higher Education*. Ms. Houston's words so well capture my life-long strategy, I want to share some of the ideas she assembled here. To that end, I have incorporated Ms.

Houston's thoughts and added some of my own comments.

What's going well? This is a better question to ask than you might think. In general, it's difficult to focus on what's going right, especially in the context of making changes. Placed in the arena of change, especially in a business setting where everyone knows the bottom line is increased revenue, people stop thinking about what's going well. When confronted with change, and the fear of loss, the human mind begins to lose scope. We narrow in on 'trouble areas' and forget that growth and change have a completely different side to them: What's going well? There is at least as much potential for growth in what's going well in an organization as there is for cutbacks in what's not.

It's an underline fact of the human condition that people lean toward complaining rather than offering praise. We're taught from a young age that when something is not right, in this case the profitability of our business, we should seek out what's wrong. This creates an unhelpful culture where criticism and competition for company resources abound. The next time you are confronted with an area of your life that needs improvement, challenge yourself by engaging in a conversation, internal or external, about what is going right. It's much more difficult than offering critique, but will lead you to a better, more affirming solution.

We can learn from the question, "What's going well?" By delving into what's going well, company culture and even underline human nature can be changed. Like many, it isn't an easy transition, but if we can discover what's seen as going well in an organization, examine the core values and habits that can often be extended from one area of a business to another, we can see dramatic improvements. What's going well in our company today? What have we been exceptionally good at over the last twelve months? As we look at taking on a new business year and reflect on the past year, what were we really effective at?

We need to get clarity on the things we are doing well, so that we can maximize the opportunities on what we are really good at. Then, and only then, we can look forward to what we can improve on in the future. Our conditioning tells us to unconsciously take for granted what we're doing well because the results are expected. I totally believe we should expect good results, but we still need to look at what we're good at because the organization needs to hear about the successes, not just the problems and the challenges.

We've all heard the old management adage, "You can't manage what you don't measure." We all know this to be true, and yet, many of our tracking systems are not up to date. If we are measuring specific results, sometimes they are not shared with the team members, unless the results need to be improved.

I recall hearing about an employee asking why his boss will not share the numbers with his staff. In truth, it is difficult to imagine why a good manager wouldn't share individual results with his staff members. People want to know where they stand. The only way we can improve a result is when we know exactly where we are today and then decide what it will take to improve to a new higher level. If we don't know where we stand today, we won't know if we improve, so what's the point? We should begin with looking at and celebrating what we are doing well, and then move on to areas of improvement. Our culture will improve, our results will improve, and our team member retention will improve.

Asking the question, "What's going well in the organization?" can also be described as being part of an organizational assessment which is a systematic process for obtaining valid information about the performance of an organization and the factors that affect performance. It differs from other types of evaluations because the assessment focuses on the organization as the primary unit of analysis.

Bertie, in the story, is new to the organization and we would expect that he will quickly want to assess the strengths of his organization. Having his team offsite for a few days will have enabled him to do a quick organizational performance and motivation assessment in some of the following areas:

Organizational Performance & Organizational Motivation

- Effectiveness History
- Efficiency Mission
- Performance Culture
- Financial Viability Incentives

Source: **Universalia** Institutional and Organizational Assessment Model (IOA Model) and the International Development Evaluation Association (IDEAS)

A key decision that any organization needs to make when undertaking an organizational assessment is whether to self-assess its performance or to commission an external assessment. Some advantages of a self-assessment are that it generally means an acceptance and an organization's ownership of the assessment, and thereby increases the latter's acceptance of feedback and commitment to the evaluation's recommendations. However, drawbacks of the self-assessment approach are that external stakeholders could question the independence or validity of the findings and fear that hard issues have not been addressed because of potential sensitivities within the organization.

Organizational assessment results have a wide variety of uses. For instance, they can be used by an organization to build its capacity, to validate its work, to promote dialog with funders or partners and to help devise its strategies for the future. However, to ensure that results of the organizational assessment are used, their use must be planned for by the organization from the onset of the assessment, as well as considered throughout the implementation phase, and even once reports have been submitted and disseminated.

Some conditions of the organizational assessment which enhance the utilization of the results are when:

- Internal leadership is identified to champion the process and results of the assessment.
- The organizational culture is one that supports use of positive and negative feedback.
- Stakeholders are involved in the assessment process.
- There is a process in place and resources allocated to implement and follow-up on the assessment's recommendations.

- Recommendations are realistic and feasible.
- When Bertie looks at his organization, he will have to review over time each of his leaders and key team players in the organization and ask the question, is this team capable of growing the business? He will also need to assess his own capabilities as well as those of his employees and management.

Assessing Bertie: The business going forward will be a direct reflection on who Bertie is. He will need to personally examine both his negative and positive qualities, to determine his impact as a leader and manager at Barkers.
- What are his strengths and weaknesses?
- How can he improve his skills to better manage the Barkers business?

Assessing Bertie's management team: An ideal management for Bertie is one that has members with diverse skills that complement each other and work well as a business unit. This will help achieve the vision of the Barkers business. It is possible to assess the value of the management team by asking the following questions:
- What does each member bring to the team?
- Do their strengths and weaknesses create a strong balance in the team?

Assessing Bertie's employees: Employees are a crucial aspect of the business. Bertie needs people who have the vitality of the business and the personality to drive the business forward.
- Do the Barkers employees know what is expected of them?

- Does Bertie have the 'right employees,' ones who contribute to making the business run smoothly?
- Is Bertie forced to rely on a small number of key people to get the work done?
- How long have the key people been in their current positions?
- Does Bertie know his employees' strengths and weaknesses?
- Bertie will need to assess each of his senior people's abilities such as business acumen, business development capabilities, product and services knowledge, technology and presentation skills, time management skills, business tracking capabilities, and business planning skills.

Asking the question, "What can we do to improve our business and *Grow* in the future?" can also be described as being the opportunity for the organization's management to voice their opinion on what needs to be changed or improved to grow the business in the future. We can only imagine the lists of suggestions that were provided in the Barkers meeting. Some could possibly be introduced quickly and inexpensively to get fast results, and yet others would need to be reviewed and discussed extensively before an implementation plan could be anticipated.

One very positive aspect is that the management team at Barkers have brought forward the list of actions to grow the business and therefore very much support and stand behind the ideas and plans. A situation which helps Bertie have a very early assessment of what needs to be done in his first 100 days as CEO of Barkers.

51 Ideas for Improving Business

The list of suggestions coming from the question, "What can we do to improve our business and *Grow* in the future?" will more than likely mirror actions being proposed in many medium size companies today. The author has researched the internet to come up with a list of 51 actions to make a business grow. This is not an exhaustive list and not all will apply to any one company. The reason for listing the ideas is to challenge the reader of this book to think about them, and perhaps at least one of the ideas may become helpful in growing a (or your) business.

There are numerous possibilities to grow a business. The first 10 ideas listed here are recommended by Karen E. Spaeder, a freelance business writer in Southern California.
Choosing a proper one (or ones) for your business will depend on the type of business you own or run, the available resources, and how much money, time and sweat equity you're willing to invest if you're ready to grow.

1. Open another location. This might not be your best choice for business expansion, but it's listed first here because that's what often comes to mind first for so many entrepreneurs considering expansion. "Physical expansion isn't always the best growth answer without careful research, planning and number-planning," says business speaker, writer and consultant Frances McGuckin, who offers the following tips for anyone considering another location:

• Make sure you're maintaining a consistent bottom-line profit and that you've shown steady growth over the past few years.

• Look at the trends, both economic and consumer, for indications on your company's staying power.

• Make sure your administrative systems and management team are extraordinary-you'll need them to get a new location up and running.

• Prepare a complete business plan for a new location.

• Determine where and how you'll obtain financing.

• Choose your location based on what's best for your business, not your wallet.

2. Offer your business as a franchise or business opportunity. Bette Fetter, founder and owner of Young Rembrandts , an Elgin, Illinois-based drawing program for children, waited 10 years to begin franchising her concept in 2001-but for Fetter and her husband, Bill, the timing was perfect. Raising four young children and keeping the business local was enough for the couple until their children grew older and they decided it was time to expand nationally.

"We chose franchising as the vehicle for expansion because we wanted an operating system that would allow ownership on the part of the staff operating Young Rembrandts locations in markets outside our home territory," says Bette. "When people have a vested interest in their work, they enjoy it more, bring more to the table and are more successful overall. Franchising is a perfect system to accomplish those goals."

Streamlining their internal systems and marketing in nearby states helped the couple bring in their first few franchisees. With seven units and some time under their belt, they then signed on with two national franchise broker firms. Now with 30 franchisees nationwide, they're staying true to their vision of steady growth. "Before we began franchising, we were teaching 2,500 children in the Chicago market," says Bette. "Today we teach more than 9,000 children nationwide, and that number will continue to grow dramatically as we grow our franchise system."

Bette advises networking within the franchise community-become a member of the International Franchise Association and find a good franchise attorney as well as a mentor who's been through the franchise process. "You need to be open to growing and expanding your vision," Bette says, "but at the same time, be a strong leader who knows how to keep the key vision in focus at all times."

3. License your product. This can be an effective, low-cost growth medium, particularly if you have a service product or branded product, notes Larry Bennett, director of the Larry Friedman International Center for Entrepreneurship at Johnson & Wales University in Providence, Rhode Island. "You can receive upfront monies and royalties from the continued sales or use of your software, name brand, etc., if it's successful," he says. Licensing also minimizes your risk and is low cost in comparison to the price of starting your own company to produce and sell your brand or product.

To find a licensing partner, start by researching companies that provide products or services similar to yours. "[But] before you set up a meeting or contact any company, find a competent attorney who specializes in intellectual property rights," advises Bennett. "This is the best way to minimize the risk of losing control of your service or product."

4. Form an alliance. Aligning yourself with a similar type of business can be a powerful way to expand quickly. Jim Labadie purchased a CD seminar set from a fellow fitness professional, Ryan Lee, on how to make and sell fitness information products. It was a move that proved lucrative for Labadie, who at the time was running an upscale personal training firm he'd founded. "What I learned on [Lee's] CDs allowed me to develop my products and form alliances within the industry," says Labadie, who now teaches business skills to fitness professionals via a series of products he created and sells on his Web site, HowToGetMoreClients.com.

Seeing that Labadie had created some well-received products of his own, Lee agreed to promote Labadie's product to his long contact list of personal trainers. "That resulted in a decent amount of sales," says Labadie-in fact, he's increased sales 500 percent since he created and started selling the products. "Plus, there have been other similar alliances I've formed with other trainers and Web sites that sell my products for a commission."

If the thought of shelling out commissions or any of your own money for the sake of an alliance makes you uncomfortable, Labadie advises looking at the big picture: "If you want to keep all the money to yourself, you're really shooting yourself in the foot," says the Tampa, Florida, entrepreneur. "You need to align with other businesses that already have lists of prospective customers. It's the fastest way to success."

5. Diversify. Small-business consultant McGuckin offers several ideas for diversifying your product or service line:
- Sell complementary products or services
- Teach adult education or other types of classes
- Import or export yours or others' products

- Become a paid speaker or columnist

"Diversifying is an excellent growth strategy, as it allows you to have multiple streams of income that can often fill seasonal voids and, of course, increase sales and profit margins," says McGuckin, who diversified from an accounting, tax and consulting business to speaking, writing and publishing.

Diversifying was always in the works for Darien, Connecticut, entrepreneurs Rebecca Cutler and Jennifer Krane, creators of the "raising a racquet" line of maternity tennis wear. "We had always planned to expand into other 'thematic' kits, consistent with our philosophies of versatility, style, health and fun," says Cutler. "Once we'd begun to establish a loyal wholesale customer base and achieve some retail brand recognition, we then broadened our product base with two line extensions, 'raising a racquet golf' and 'raising a racquet yoga.'"

Rolling out the new lines last year allowed the partners' current retail outlets to carry more of their inventory. "It also broadened our target audience and increased our presence in the marketplace, giving us the credibility to approach much larger retailers," notes Cutler, who expects to double their sales and further diversify the company's product lines. "As proof, we've recently been selected by Bloomingdale's, A Pea in the Pod and Mimi Maternity."

6. Target other markets. Your current market is serving you well. Are there others? You bet. "My other markets are what make money for me," says McGuckin. Electronic and foreign rights, entrepreneurship programs, speaking events and software offerings produce multiple revenue streams for McGuckin, from multiple markets.

"If your consumer market ranges from teenagers to college students, think about where these people spend most of their time," says McGuckin. "Could you introduce your business to schools, clubs or colleges? You could offer discounts to special-interest clubs or donate part of [your profits] to schools and associations."

Baby boomers, elderly folks, teens, tweens...let your imagination take you where you need to be. Then take your product to the markets that need it.

7. Win a government contract. "The best way for a small business to grow is to have the federal government as a customer," wrote Rep. Nydia M. Velazquez, ranking Democratic member of the House Small Business Committee. "The U.S. government is the largest buyer of goods and services in the world, with total procurement dollars reaching over $235 billion."

Working with your local SBA and SBDC offices as well as the Service Corps of Retired Executives and your local, regional or state Economic Development Agency will help you determine the types of contracts available to you. The U.S. Chamber of Commerce and the SBA also have a Business Matchmaking Program designed to match entrepreneurs with buyers. "A fair amount of patience is required in working to secure most government contracts," says Johnson & Wales University's Bennett. "Requests for proposals usually require a significant amount of groundwork and research. If you're not prepared to take the time to fully comply with RFP terms and conditions, you'll only be wasting your time."

This might sound like a lot of work, but it could be worth it: "The good part about winning government contracts," says Bennett, "is that once you've jumped through the hoops and win a bid, you're generally not subject to the level of external competition of the outside marketplaces."

8. Merge with or acquire another business. In 1996, when Mark Fasciano founded FatWire , a Mineola, New York, content management software company, he certainly couldn't have predicted what would happen a few years later. Just as FatWire was gaining market momentum, the tech downturn hit hard. "We were unable to generate the growth needed to maximize the strategic partnerships we'd established with key industry players," Fasciano says. "During this tech 'winter,' we concentrated on survival and servicing our clients, while searching for an opportunity to jump-start the company's growth. That growth opportunity came last year at the expense of one of our competitors."

Scooping up the bankrupt company, divine Inc., from the auction block was the easy part; then came the integration of the two companies. "The process was intense and exhausting," says Fasciano, who notes four keys to their success:

- Customer retention - "I personally spoke with 150 customers within the first few weeks of consummating the deal, and I met with 45 clients around the globe in the first six months," notes Fasciano. They've retained 95 percent of the divine Inc. customer base.
- Staff retention - Fasciano rehired the best and brightest of divine's staff.
- Melding technologies - "One of the reasons I was so confident about this acquisition was the two product architectures were very similar," says Fasciano. This allowed for a smooth integration of the two technologies.

• Focus - "Maybe the biggest reason this acquisition has worked so well is the focus that FatWire has brought to a neglected product," says Fasciano.

FatWire's acquisition of divine grew its customer base from 50 to 400, and the company grew 150 percent, from $6 million to $15 million.

9. Expand globally. Not only did FatWire grow in terms of customers and sales, it also experienced global growth simply as a result of integrating the best of the divine and FatWire technologies. "FatWire finally has international reach-we've established new offices in the United Kingdom, France, Italy, Spain, Holland, Germany, China, Japan and Singapore," says Fasciano. This increased market share is what will allow FatWire to realize sustained growth.

But you don't need to acquire another business to expand globally. You just need to prime your offering for an international market the way FatWire was primed following the integration of its technologies with divine's.

You'll also need a foreign distributor who'll carry an inventory of your product and resell it in their domestic markets. You can locate foreign distributors by scouring your city or state for a foreign company with a U.S. representative. Trade groups, foreign chambers of commerce in the United States, and branches of American chambers of commerce in foreign countries are also good places to find distributors you can work with.

10. Expand to the Internet. "Bill Gates said that by the end of 2002, there will be only two kinds of businesses: those with an Internet presence, and those with no business at all," notes Sally Falkow a Pasadena, California, Web content strategist. "Perhaps this was overstating the case, but an effective Web site is an integral part of business today."

Landing your Web site in search engine results is key-more than 80 percent of traffic comes via search engines, according to Falkow. "As there are now more than 4 billion Web pages and traffic on the Internet doubles every 100 days, making your Web site visible is vital," she says. "You need every weapon you can get."

Design and programming are also important, but it's your content that will draw a visitor into your site and get them to stay. Says Falkow, "Putting together a content strategy based on user behavior, measuring and tracking visitor click streams, and writing the content based on researched keywords will get you excellent search results and meet the needs of your visitors."

And here are another 41 growth ideas the author can vouch for, selected from an article in *Reader's Digest*:

11. Be a more efficient time manager by using the rule of two. Focus on the two most important tasks in your day, and you'll become more productive.

12. Start a filing system and toss everything you don't need. Eliminating will make it easier to locate the important papers.

13. Limit your work-starting routine to 15 minutes. That is, don't spend more than 15 minutes getting coffee, settling in, reading e-mails, checking messages, or looking at newspapers. You are often at your freshest and most productive at the beginning of the day.

14. Write two to-do lists. The first should contain everything that you need to get done soon. It should be a comprehensive list of short-, medium-, and long-term projects and work, and you should constantly adjust it. The second to-do list should be what you can reasonably expect to get done today, and today only.

15. Schedule some reading time. There's not a job that doesn't require at least some reading, be it about the company, the industry, the marketplace, the economy, the price of tomatoes, etc.

16. Embrace the number one truth about stress: Only you create it. Take some deep breaths. Make a list of everything that needs to get done. It will help you to organize your day.

17. Every night before bed, take five minutes to look over the day ahead. This brief look into the future will help you feel more prepared in the morning.

18. Take on just one new activity at a time. When you try to master too many new activities at once, you can easily feel overwhelmed.

19. Carry a small notebook with you everywhere. This is your "worry" journal. When you feel stressed, whip it out and scribble down everything on your mind at that minute.

20. Take breaks throughout the day. It will help clear your mind and relieve pressure. Something as simple as going to the water cooler for a drink may do the trick.

21. Use a monthly calendar for short-term scheduling and a 6-month calendar for long-range scheduling. Pencil in all things that pertain to your goals, including classes you want to take, regular exercise sessions, social events, and family time.

22. On a daily action list, categorize tasks: those that need immediate attention (you had better do them yourself), those that can be delegated, and those that can be put off. To avoid procrastination, tackle the toughest jobs first, breaking them into smaller, less daunting components.

23. Free up time for the things you really want to do by simplifying your life. Let go of activities that don't contribute to your goals.

24. Reduce the waste—and frustration—of everyday delays. Wherever you go, take reading material or a portable music player. Then when you have to wait, you can make good use of or enjoy the time.

25. Be patient. Said one mom and wife: "I wanted everything done my way. I was unwilling to let go of any part of it until it was perfect. So I've had to learn to slow down. After a few years, I finally get it: Nothing happens overnight."

26. Make a point of sharing your knowledge with young professionals as well as high-level executives. Both will remember you for your time and consideration.

27. Keep abreast of trends in your industry by joining professional associations, attending conferences, and reading newsletters and magazines. Take classes and attend training to learn from others in your field.

28. Make networking with others in your field a priority. Schedule some time to meet for coffee or lunch or keep in touch via email and social networks.

29. Learn the importance of giving yourself pep talks, and keep the voice in your head positive. Stay focused, and be willing to work as hard as you need to.

30. Try to challenge yourself in new ways. Seek out complex work and new ideas to avoid boredom and repetition.

31. Take care of your health. Schedule that physical exam you've been putting off and make sure you get exercise and take care of any personal issues that are troubling you.

32. Keep positive. Hold the big picture in your sights. What's gloomy for one can be a gold mine for another.

33. Reinvent. Create new products or services—or reconfigure old ones. Implement solutions that are valuable to your key customers.

34. Don't do it alone! Get support from family, friends, coaches, and fellow entrepreneurs.

35. Perform an assessment of the market conditions to find out how you match up to other companies like yours, get clear on your financial position.

36. Get input from your employees and customers or clients. They probably have a lot of ideas for how you could grow, and it might not have occurred to you to ask them.

37. Project a consistent polished professional image, in order to send the message to the world that the quality of your product and/or service.

38. Make a list with categories like, what must get done; would you like to get done, what can wait until another time.

39. Take a step back and learn how to delegate. A great mantra is, "Don't just do it, delegate it!"

40. Develop a brand identity which will resonate with the customer and reflect the key aspects of the company, including not only its products, but its culture and goals.

41. Be a visionary. Picture what you would like your business to be like.

42. Be committed to excellence. There will always be bumps in the road. It is a part of life and it is a part of business. The true test is how you and your company deal with them.

43. Be innovative. Find innovative solutions to solve your problems. There are a million ways to grow your business. Find the smart, innovative ways that are best for you.

44. Embrace your mistakes and learn from them.

45. Realize that failures are merely steps in our progress. For example, Thomas Edison made over 10,000 light bulbs before he made one that actually worked.

46. Luck is the marriage of opportunity with preparedness. You obviously have the attitude part prepared—so the rest is actually doing the basic steps that lead to greatness.

47. Raise your prices. When pricing most business owners research their market, look at what their competition is charging and find a happy medium between them.

48. Find a target market that is willing to pay for premium prices. The luxury market is booming and every business should find a product to serve them.

49. Three ways to grow any business: Get more clients; sell existing clients more often; and sell existing clients more stuff.

50. Collaboration. Whether it is bartering or partnering with someone else, find the people who have what you need and are willing to collaborate with you. A true WIN/WIN situation can skyrocket a business!

51. Take a few moments to assess the day's emotional challenges. Almost as important as your to-do list is a 'be prepared for' list. Inventory the tough phone calls, boring meetings, challenging customers, frustrating red tape, infuriating rush-hour drives, droning detail work, and other challenges you may face.

BUSINESS GROWTH: A DEFINITION FROM THE BD BUSINESS DIRECTORY

The process of improving some measure of an enterprise's success, business growth can be achieved either by boosting the top line of revenue of the business with greater product sales or service income, or by increasing the bottom line or profitability of the operation by minimizing costs.

CONCLUSION

Earlier in this book I described how I was persuaded by friends and past employees to put on paper some of the management tools I had developed and used in my career at different organizations around the world. What I have not said, until now, is what drove me to use this particular style of writing and story-telling, involving the Barkers characters in this book.

It was about twenty years ago that I was given a copy of the book *Who Moved My Cheese*, written by Spencer Johnson and published by GP Putnam's Sons. The book is about four characters; *Sniff* and *Scurry*, the mice, and two little people, human metaphors, *Hem* and *Haw*. The *Hem* and *Haw* descriptions are the names of the little people, taken from the phrase hem-and-haw, a term of indecisiveness. The book is about change and uses a fable about *Sniff* and *Scurry* and *Hem* and *Haw* to weave a story about reaction to change, an occurrence which we all know is inevitable. However, we also all know change is a little hard to accept at times.

After reading this book, I had the idea that if I ever wrote a book about managing people and business, I would use a similar style to try to get points across to my audience. I truly hope you enjoyed reading Barkers and that you found some helpful hints to guide you in your business, and also in the way you interact with people in your business life.

John Costin

REFERENCES

Books:

Johnson, Spencer. *Who Moved My Cheese?: An A-Mazing Way to Deal with Change in Your Work and in Your Life*. 1st ed. New York: G. P. Putnam's Sons, 1998. Print.

Websites:

Business Directory. Business Growth: A Definition from the BD Business Directory. *Businessdictionary.com*. http://www.businessdictionary.com/definition/profit.html

Houston, Natalie. What's Going Well? *Chronicle.com*. http://www.chronicle.com/blogs/profhacker/whats-going-well/39120

Institutional and Organizational Performance Assessment. *Universalia.com*. http://www.universalia.com/en/services/institutional-and-organizational-performance-assessment

Reader's Digest Editors. 46 Tips to Help Improve Your Business. *Rd.com*. http://www.rd.com/advice/work-career/46-tips-to-help-improve-your-business/

Spaeder, Karen E. 10 Ways to Grow Your Business. *Entrepreneur.com*. https://www.entrepreneur.com/article/70660

John Costin

www.johncostin.com

73990059R00099

Made in the USA
Columbia, SC
25 July 2017